Smee & Other Short Stories by AM Burrage

Alfred McLelland Burrage was born in Hillingdon, Middlesex on 1st July, 1889. His father and uncle were both writers, primarily of boy's fiction, and by age 16 AM Burrage had joined them. The young man had ambitions to write for the adult market too. The money was better and so was his writing.

From 1890 to 1914, prior to the mainstream appeal of cinema and radio the printed word, mainly in magazines, was the foremost mass entertainment. AM Burrage quickly became a master of the market publishing his stories regularly across a number of publications. By the start of the Great War Burrage was well established but in 1916 he was conscripted to fight on the Western Front. He continued to write during these years documenting his experiences in the classic book War is War by Ex-Private X.

For the remainder of his life Burrage was rarely printed in book form but continued to write and be published on a prodigious scale in magazines and newspapers. In this volume we concentrate on his supernatural stories which are, by common consent, some of the best ever written. Succinct yet full of character each reveals a twist and a flavour that is unsettling.....sometimes menacing....always disturbing.

There are many other volumes available in this series together with a number of audiobooks. All are available from iTunes, Amazon and other fine digital stores.

Table Of Contents

Smee

'No,' said Jackson, with a deprecatory smile, 'I'm sorry. I don't want to upset your game. I shan't be doing that because you'll have plenty without me. But I'm not playing any games of hide-and-seek.'

It was Christmas Eve, and we were a party of fourteen with just the proper leavening of youth. We had dined well; it was the season for childish games; and we were all in the mood for playing them—all, that is, except Jackson. When somebody suggested hide-and-seek there was rapturous and almost unanimous approval. His was the one dissentient voice.

It was not like Jackson to spoil sport or refuse to do as others wanted. Somebody asked him if he were feeling seedy.

'No,' he answered, 'I feel perfectly fit, thanks. But,' he added with a smile which softened without retracting the flat refusal, 'I'm not playing hide-and-seek.'

One of us asked him why not. He hesitated for some seconds before replying.

'I sometimes go and stay at a house where a girl was killed through playing hide-and-seek in the dark. She didn't know the house very well. There was a servants' staircase with a door to it. When she was pursued she opened the door and jumped into what she must have thought was one of the bedrooms—and she broke her neck at the bottom of the stairs.'

We all looked concerned, and Mrs Femley said:

'How awful! And you were there when it happened?'

Jackson shook his head very gravely.

'No,' he said, 'but I was there when something else happened. Something worse.'

'I shouldn't have thought anything could be worse.'

'This was,' said Jackson and shuddered visibly. 'Or so it seemed to me.'

I think he wanted to tell the story and was angling for encouragement. A few requests, which may have seemed to him to lack urgency, he affected to ignore and went off at a tangent.

'I wonder if any of you have played a game called "Smee"? It's a great improvement on the ordinary game of hide-and-seek. The name derives from the ungrammatical colloquialism, "It's me". You might care to play if you're going to play a game of that sort. Let me tell you the rules.

'Every player is presented with a sheet of paper. All the sheets are blank except one, on which is written "Smee". Nobody knows who is "Smee" except "Smee" himself—or herself as the case may be. The lights are then turned out and "Smee" slips from the room and goes off to hide, and after an interval the other players go off in search, without knowing whom they are actually in search of. One player meeting another challenges with the word Smee", and the other player, if not the one concerned, answers "Smee".

'The real "Smee" makes no answer when challenged, and the second player remains quietly by him. Presently they will be discovered by a third player who, having challenged and received no answer, will link up with the first two. This goes on until all the players have formed a chain, and the last to join it is marked down for a forfeit. It's a good noisy, romping game, and in a big house it often takes a long time to complete the chain. You might care to try it; and I'll pay my forfeit and smoke one of Tim's excellent cigars here by the fire, until you get tired of it.'

I remarked that it sounded a good game and asked Jackson if he had played it himself.

'Yes,' he answered, 'I played it in the house I was telling you about.'

'And she was there? The girl who broke'

'No, no,' Mrs Femley interrupted. 'He told us he wasn't there when it happened.'

Jackson considered.

'I don't know if she were there or not. I'm afraid she was. I know that there were thirteen of us and there ought only to have been twelve. And I'll swear that I didn't know her name, or I think I should have gone clean off my head when I heard that whisper in the dark. No, you don't catch me playing that game, or any other like it, any more. It spoilt my nerve quite a while, and I can't afford to take long holidays. Besides, it saves a lot of trouble and inconvenience to own up at once to being a coward.'

Tim Vouce, the best of hosts, smiled around at us, and in that smile there was a meaning which is sometimes vulgarly expressed by the slow closing of an eye. 'There's a story coming,' he announced.

'There's certainly a story of sorts,' said Jackson, 'but whether it's coming or not'

He paused and shrugged his shoulders.

'Well, you're going to pay a forfeit instead of playing?'

'Please. But have a heart and let me down lightly. It's a not just sheer cussedness on my part.'

'Payment in advance,' said Tim, 'ensures honesty and promotes good feeling. You are therefore sentenced to tell the story here and now.'

And here follows Jackson's story, unrevised by me and passed on without comment to a wider public:

Some of you, I know, have run across the Sangstons. Christopher Sangston and his wife, I mean. They're distant connections of mine—at least, Violet Sangston is. About eight years ago they bought a house between the North and South Downs on the Surrey and Sussex border, and five years ago they invited me to come and spend Christmas with them.

It was a fairly old house—I couldn't say exactly of what period—and it certainly deserved the epithet 'rambling'. It wasn't a particularly big house, but the original architect, whoever he may have been, had not concerned himself with economising in space, and at first you could get lost in it quite easily.

Well, I went down for that Christmas, assured by Violet's letter that I knew most of my fellow guests and that the two or three who might be strangers to me were all 'lambs'. Unfortunately I'm one of the world's workers, and I couldn't get away until Christmas Eve, although the other members of the party had assembled on the preceding day. Even then I had to cut it rather fine to be there for dinner on my first night. They were all dressing when I arrived and I had to go straight to my room and waste no time. I may even have kept dinner waiting for a bit, for I was last down, and it was announced within a minute of my entering the drawing-room. There was just time to say 'hullo' to everybody I knew, to be briefly introduced to the two or three I didn't know, and then I had to give my arm to Mrs Gorman.

I mention this as the reason why I didn't catch the name of a tall, dark, handsome girl I hadn't met before. Everything was rather hurried and I am always bad at catching people's names. She looked cold and clever and rather forbidding, the sort of girl who gives the impression of knowing all about men and the more she knows of them the less she likes them. I felt that I wasn't going to hit it off with this particular iamb' of Violet's, but she looked interesting all the same, and I wondered who she was. I didn't ask, because I was pretty sure of hearing somebody address her by name before very long.

Unluckily, though, I was a long way off her at table, and as Mrs Gorman was at the top of her form that night I soon forgot to worry about who she might be. Mrs Gorman is one of the most amusing women I know, an outrageous but quite innocent flirt, with a very sprightly wit which isn't always unkind. She can think half a dozen moves ahead in conversation just as an expert can in a game of chess. We were soon sparring, or, rather, I was 'covering' against the ropes, and I quite forgot to ask her in an undertone the name of the cold, proud beauty. The lady on the other side of me was a stranger, or had been until a few minutes since, and I didn't think of seeking information in that quarter.

There was a round dozen of us, including the Sangstons themselves, and we were all young or trying to be. The Sangstons themselves were the oldest members of the party, and their son Reggie, in his last year at Marlborough, must have been the youngest. When there was talk of playing games after dinner it was he who suggested 'Smee'. He told us how to play it just as I've described it to you.

His father chipped in as soon as we all understood what was going to be required of us.

'If there are any games of that sort going on in the house,' he said, 'for goodness' sake be careful of the back stairs on the first floor landing. There's a door to them and I've often meant to take it down. In the dark anybody who doesn't know the house very well might think they were walking into a room. A girl actually did break her neck on those stairs about ten years ago when the Ainsties lived here.'

I asked how it happened.

'Oh,' said Sangston, 'there was a party here one Christmas time and they were playing hide-and-seek as you propose doing. This girl was one of the hiders. She heard somebody coming, ran along the passage to get away, and opened the door of what she thought was a bedroom, evidently with the intention of hiding behind it while her pursuer went past. Unfortunately it was the door leading to the back stairs, and that staircase is as straight and almost as steep as the shaft of a pit. She was dead when they picked her up.'

We all promised for our own sakes to be careful. Mrs Gorman said that she was sure nothing could happen to her, since she was insured by three different newspapers and her next of kin was a brother whose consistent ill-luck was a by-word in the family. You see, none of us had known the unfortunate girl, and as the tragedy was ten years old there was no need to pull long faces about it.

Well, we started the game almost immediately after dinner. The men allowed themselves only five minutes before joining the ladies, and then young Reggie Sangston went round and assured himself that the lights were out all over the house except in the servants' quarters and in the drawing-room where we were assembled. He then got busy with twelve sheets of paper which he twisted into pellets and shook up between his hands before passing them round. Eleven of them were blank, and 'Smee' was written on the twelfth. The person drawing the latter was the one who had to hide. I looked and saw that mine was a blank. A moment later out went the electric lights, and in the darkness I heard somebody get up and creep to the door.

After a minute or so somebody gave a signal and we made a rush for the door. I for one hadn't the least idea which of the party was 'Smee'. For five or ten minutes we were all rushing up and down passages and in and out rooms challenging one another and answering, 'Smee?—Smee!'

After a bit the alarums and excursions died down, and I guessed that 'Smee' was found. Eventually I found a chain of people all sitting still and holding their breath on some narrow stairs leading up to a row of attics. I hastily joined it, having challenged and been answered with silence, and presently two more stragglers arrived each racing the other to avoid being last. Sangston was one of them, indeed it was he who was marked down for a forfeit, and after a little while he remarked in an undertone, i think we're all here now, aren't we?'

He struck a match, looked up the shaft of the staircase, and began to count. It wasn't hard, although we just about filled the staircase, for we were sitting each a step or two one above the next, and all our heads were visible. '. . . nine, ten, eleven, twelve—thirteen,' he concluded, and then laughed.

'Dash it all, that's one too many!'

The match had burnt out and he struck another and began again to count.

He got as far as twelve, and then uttered an exclamation.

'There are thirteen people here!' he exclaimed, 'I haven't counted myself yet.'

'Oh, nonsense!' I laughed. 'You probably began with yourself, and now you want to count yourself twice.'

Out came his son's electric torch, giving a brighter and steadier light and we all began to count. Of course we numbered twelve. Sangston laughed.

'Well,' he said, i could have sworn I counted thirteen twice.'

From half way up the stairs came Violet Sangston's voice with a little nervous trill in it.

'I thought there was somebody sitting two steps above me. Have you moved up, Captain Ransome?'

Ransome said that he hadn't. He also said that he thought there was somebody sitting between Violet and himself. Just for a moment there was an uncomfortable Something in the air, a little cold ripple which touched us all. For that little moment it seemed to all of us, I think, that something odd and unpleasant had happened and was liable to happen again. Then we laughed at ourselves and at one another and were comfortable once more. There were only twelve of us, and there could only have been twelve of us, and there was no argument about it. Still laughing we trooped back to the drawing-room to begin again.

This time I was 'Smee', and Violet Sangston ran me to earth while I was still looking for a hiding-place. That round didn't last long, and we were a chain of twelve within two or three minutes. Afterwards there was a short interval. Violet wanted a wrap fetched for her, and her husband went up to get it from her room. He was no sooner gone than Reggie pulled me by the sleeve. I saw that he was looking pale and sick.

'Quick!' he whispered, 'while father's out of the way. Take me into the smoke-room and give me a brandy or a whisky or something. You know the sort of dose a fellow ought to have.'

Outside the room I asked him what was the matter, but he didn't answer at first, and I thought it better to dose him first and question him afterwards.

So I mixed him a pretty dark-complexioned brandy and soda which he drank at a gulp and then began to puff as if he had been running, 'I've had rather a turn,' he said to me with a sheepish grin.

'What's the matter?'

'I don't know. You were "Smee" just now, weren't you? Well, of course I didn't know who "Smee" was, and while mother and the others ran into the west wing and found you, I turned east. There's a deep clothes cupboard in my bedroom—I'd marked it down as a good place to hide when it was my turn, and I had an idea that "Smee" might be there. I opened the door in the dark, felt round, and touched somebody's hand. " 'Smee'?" I whispered, and not getting any answer I thought I had found "Smee".

'Well, I don't know how it was, but an odd creepy feeling came over me. I can't describe it, but I felt that something was wrong. So I turned on my electric torch and there was nobody there. Now I swear I touched a hand, and I was filling up the doorway of the cupboard at the time, so nobody could get out and past me.' He puffed again. 'What do you make of it?' he asked.

'You imagined that you touched a hand,' I answered, naturally enough.

He uttered a short laugh. 'Of course I knew you were going to say that,' he said, I must have imagined it, mustn't I?' He paused and swallowed, i mean, it couldn't have been anything else but imagination, could it?' I assured him that it couldn't, meaning what I said, and he accepted this, but rather with the philosophy of one who knows he is right but doesn't expect to be believed. We returned together to the drawing-room where, by that time, they were all waiting for us and ready to start again.

It may have been my imagination—although I'm almost sure it wasn't—but it seemed to me that all enthusiasm for the game had suddenly melted like a white frost in strong sunlight. If anybody had suggested another game I'm sure we should all have been grateful and abandoned 'Smee'. Only nobody did. Nobody seemed to like to. I for one, and I can speak for some of the others, too, was oppressed with the feeling that there was something wrong. I couldn't have said what I thought was wrong, indeed I didn't think about it at all, but somehow all the sparkle had gone out of the fun, and hovering over my mind like a shadow was the warning of some sixth sense which told me that there was an influence in the house which was neither sane, sound nor healthy. Why did I feel like that? Because Sangston had counted thirteen of us instead of twelve, and his son had thought he had touched somebody in an empty cupboard. No, there was more in it than just that. One would have laughed at such things in the ordinary way, and it was just that feeling of something being wrong which stopped me from laughing. Well, we started again, and when we went in pursuit of the unknown 'Smee', we were as noisy as ever, but it seemed to me that most of us were acting. Frankly, for no reason other than the one I've given you, we'd stopped enjoying the game. I had an instinct to hunt with the main pack, but after a few minutes, during which no 'Smee' had been found, my instinct to play winning games and be first if possible, set me searching on my own account. And on the first floor of the west wing, followed the wall which was actually the shell of the house, I blundered against a pair of human knees.

I put out my hand and touched a soft, heavy curtain. Then I knew where I was. There were tall, deeply-recessed windows with seats along the landing, and curtains over the recesses to the ground. Somebody was sitting in a comer of this window-seat behind the curtain.

Aha, I had caught 'Smee'! So I drew the curtain aside, stepped in, and touched the bare arm of a woman. It was a dark night outside, and moreover the window was not only curtained but a blind hung down to where the bottom panes joined up with the frame. Between (he curtain and the window it was as dark as the plague of Egypt. I could not have seen my hand held six inches before my face, much less the woman sitting in the corner.

'Smee?' I whispered.

I had no answer. 'Smee' when challenged does not answer. So I sat down beside her, first in the field, to await the others. Then, having settled myself I leaned over to her and whispered:

'Who is it? What's your name, "Smee"?'

And out of the darkness beside me the whisper came back: 'Brenda Ford.'

I didn't know the name, but because I didn't know it I guessed at once who she was. The tall, pale, dark girl was the only person in the house I didn't know by name. Ergo my companion was the tall, pale, dark girl. It seemed rather intriguing to be there with her, shut in between a heavy curtain and a window, and I rather wondered whether she was enjoying the game we were all playing. Somehow she hadn't seemed to me to be one of the romping sort. I muttered one or two commonplace questions to her and had no answer.

'Smee' is a game of silence. 'Smee' and the person or persons who have found 'Smee' are supposed to keep quiet to make it hard for the others. But there was nobody else about, and it occurred to me that she was playing the game a little too much to the letter. I spoke again and got no answer, and then I began to be annoyed. She was of that cold, 'superior' type which affects to despise men; she didn't like me; and she was sheltering behind the rules of a game for children to be discourteous. Well, if she didn't like sitting there with me, I certainly didn't want to be sitting there with her! I half turned from her and began to hope that we should both be discovered without much more delay.

Having discovered that I didn't like being there alone with her, it was queer how soon I found myself hating it, and that for a reason very different from the one which had at first whetted my annoyance. The girl I had met for the first time before dinner, and seen diagonally across the table, had a sort of cold charm about her which attracted while it had half angered me. For the girl who was with me, imprisoned in the opaque darkness between the curtain and the window, I felt no attraction at all. It was so very much the reverse that I should have wondered at myself if, after the first shock of the discovery that she had suddenly become repellent to me, I had no room in my mind for anything besides the consciousness that her close presence was an increasing horror to me.

It came upon me just as quickly as I've uttered the words. My flesh suddenly shrank from her as you see a strip of gelatine shrink and wither before the heat of a fire. That feeling of something being wrong had come back to me, but multiplied to an extent which turned foreboding into actual terror. I firmly believe that I should have got up and run if I had not felt that at my first movement she would have divined my intention and compelled me to stay, by some means of which I could not bear to think. The memory of having touched her bare arm made me wince and draw in my lips. I prayed that somebody else would come along soon.

My prayer was answered. Light footfalls sounded on the landing. Somebody on the other side of the curtain brushed against my knees. The curtain was drawn aside and a woman's hand, fumbling in the darkness, presently rested on my shoulder. I "Smee"?' whispered a voice which I instantly recognized as Mrs Gorman's.

Of course she received no answer. She came and settled down beside me with a rustle, and I can't describe the sense of relief she brought me.

'It's Tony, isn't it?' she whispered.

'Yes,' I whispered back.

'You're not "Smee" are you?'

'No, she's on my other side.'

She reached a hand across me, and I heard one of her nails scratch the surface of a woman's silk gown.

'Hullo, "Smee"! How are you? Who are you? Oh, is it against the rules to talk? Never mind. Tony, we'll break the rules. Do you know, Tony, this game is beginning to irk me a little. I hope they're not going to run it to death by playing it all the evening. I'd like to play some game where we can all be together in the same room with a nice bright fire.'

'Same here,' I agreed fervently.

'Can't you suggest something when we go down? There's something rather uncanny in this particular amusement. I can't quite shed the delusion that there's somebody in this game who oughtn't to be in at all.'

That was just how I had been feeling but I didn't say so. But for my part the worst of my qualms were now gone; the arrival of Mrs Gorman had dissipated them. We sat on talking, wondering from time to time when the rest of the party would arrive.

I don't know how long elapsed before we heard a clatter of feet on the landing and young Reggie's voice shouting, 'Hullo! Hullo, there! Anybody there?'

'Yes,' I answered.

'Mrs Gorman with you?'

'Yes.'

'Well, you're a nice pair! You're both forfeited. We've all been waiting for you for hours.'

'Why, you haven't found "Smee" yet,' I objected.

'You haven't, you mean. I happen to have been "Smee" myself.'

'But "Smee's" here with us,' I cried.

'Yes,' agreed Mrs Gorman.

The curtain was stripped aside and in a moment we were blinking into the eye of Reggie's electric torch. I looked at Mrs Gorman and then on my other side. Between me and the wall there was an empty space on the window seat. I stood up at once and wished I hadn't, for I found myself sick and dizzy.

'There was somebody there,' I maintained, 'because I touched her.'

'So did I,' said Mrs Gorman in a voice which had lost its steadiness.

'And I don't see how she could have got up and gone without our knowing it.'

Reggie uttered a queer, shaken laugh. He, too, had had an unpleasant experience that evening.

'Somebody's been playing the goat,' he remarked. 'Coming down?'

We were not very popular when we arrived in the drawing-room. Reggie rather tactlessly gave it out that he had found us sitting on a window-seat behind a curtain. I taxed the tall, dark girl with having pretended to be 'Smee' and afterwards slipping away. She denied it. After which we settled down and played other games. 'Smee' was done with for the evening, and I for one was glad of it.

Some long while later, during an interval Sangston told me, if I wanted a drink, to go into the smoke-room and help myself. I went, and he presently followed me. I could see that he was rather peeved with me, and the reason came out during the following minute or two. It seemed that in his opinion, if I must sit out and flirt with Mrs Gorman—in circumstances which would have been considered highly compromising in his young days—I needn't do it during a round game and keep everybody else waiting for us.

'But there was somebody else there,' I protested, 'somebody pretending to be "Smee". I believe it was that tall, dark girl, Miss Ford, although she denied it. She even whispered her name to me.'

Sangston stared at me and nearly dropped his glass.

'Miss Who?' he shouted.

'Brenda Ford—she told me her name was.'

Sangston put down his glass and laid a hand on my shoulder.

'Look here, old man,' he said, 'I don't mind a joke, but don't let it go too far. We don't want all the women in the house getting hysterical. Brenda Ford is the name of the girl who broke her neck on the stairs playing hide-and-seek here ten years ago.'

The Last of the Kerstons

I, Richard Wake, am a sane man.

I have been examined by half a score of brain specialists, and having been found sane, I am condemned to die for the murder of my best friend.

An hour ago I watched the sun go down for the last time. It was the devil who arranged that sunset. He lured me to the window with a promise of rose-coloured sky reflected on the whitewashed wall, and held back the curtains of night while I looked between the bars and feasted my eyes on the glory of the western sky. He led me back over a weary waste of years, and I was on the river with laughing girls in light summer dresses, watching just such a sky as that, listening to the stream washing in the sedges and the heavy lap of the water against the boat.

He showed me a child on the seashore clinging to its mother, and wondering where the sun would go when it had dropped behind the distant line of sea. He took me back to school, through the dear old ink-stained classrooms, and I heard the click of bats, and glad, honest, youthful laughter from the playing fields outside. And there, as I waited listening, a boy joined me with outstretched hands and friendship in his eyes, and I knew him at once as Julian Maltrey. But he faded instantly, for hard realities came crowding back, and I saw nothing but the whitewashed walls of my cell, where the light of day was already merging into sombre twilight.

Ah, Julian! can you look down and watch me die like a common cut-throat? I never failed you in life. Can you do nothing to rob the devil who killed you of his crowning act of vengeance?

What does Godfrey Kerston want with my life? Was not yours enough?

What wrong have I done him that he should hate me so?

I can write no more at present. There are strange noises in this place, just as there were at Kerston Hall after they let him in. He is here with me now. Presently I shall hear him laughing in the darkened corners of my cell.

The gaoler says it is my imagination. There is no one here. But he heard something, for I saw him shiver slightly.

How shall I tell my story? Those who will read it have not seen what I have seen, have not felt the icy hand of a nameless fear clutching their hearts as I have felt it. Had I the gift I would write this statement so that the reader should afterwards say: 'There is truth here. One can read it in every line. The poor fellow was innocent.'

But I must hurry on, for the gallows await me in the yard outside, and tomorrow morning they will rouse me early.

To begin at the beginning, I must go back a good many years. Julian and I were chums at school, where our greatest enemy was Godfrey Kerston. Julian and I were not gentlemen, and our names were so well known that we could scarcely pretend to be other than what we were. Our parents, rich, worthy, and well-meaning, were sprung from the people, and pitchforked us into an expensive public school in the hope of making us what they were not, with the risk of our becoming ashamed of them when we grew up. But we were good fellows, and this, with abundant supplies of pocket-money, helped most of the fellows to forget our humble origin. But we had one enemy—Godfrey Kerston.

I think he loathed us at first merely as representatives of our class, but a strong personal hatred was not long in coming. He was the last of an old but impoverished family, a race of blue-blooded snobs, with scarcely the means to keep his aristocratic soul in his delicate, shapely body. His mother reigned during his minority at Kerston Hall, a fine old place in the Midlands, and drew from the played-out estate rather less than sufficient to make both ends meet.

No wonder he hated us. We were sons of the people, who, backed by our vulgarly acquired money, were stepping into the shoes of such as himself. Even after years of school and 'Varsity we were never gentlemen to him. We were red-faced, clumsy bounders, of the kind that drop their aitches, and say outre things, and wear diamond rings on all their fingers.

Let me be fair. We hated him, too, and when as a boy he made veiled references to our origin in his slow, well-bred, drawling voice, we twitted him with his poverty in language that would have shocked our respective parents. He had a way of laughing when we hit him hardest which angered us more than ever. There was so much conscious superiority in that laugh, and such a sneer, that I think we could both have killed him.

As we grew older, the open warfare ceased, and the hatred that still smouldered within us rarely showed itself. At Oxford we saw a good deal of each other without belonging to the same set, and afterwards his name was on the lists of two of the clubs to which Julian and I belonged.

It is strange that we should both have been present when Godfrey Kerston met with the accident which caused his death a few hours afterwards. We were stopping at a house not far from Kerston Hall, where our host was a rabid fox-hunter. They run a famous pack in that part of the country, and we were only too willing to accept his offer of mounts during the few days of our stay with him.

Kerston was one of the first men we saw at the only meet we attended. He was mounted on a fine chestnut hunter, and riding by the side of a tall, dark girl, the daughter of a neighbouring squire. He bowed to us coldly, and turned to address some remark to the girl with a smile that curled his upper lip. We were sure he was speaking of us, and Julian's rage found vent in words for the first time since he was a fourth-form youngster.

'Curse that fellow!' he said. 'God help his pride if ever I get the chance to humble it!'

But Julian got no such chance while Kerston lived. That day we witnessed one of those terrible accidents which are of frequent occurrence in the hunting field. His horse threw him after taking a hedge, and rolled on him.

Julian and I were first on the spot. To do us justice, we felt nothing but horror and regret as we took up the mangled thing that had once been Kerston and laid it on a hurdle. They carried him back to his mother, and on the evening of that same day he died.

God forgive us if we had any spite against the dead. We have paid dearly enough. We might still have been living, happy, free, prosperous, had not some devil prompted Julian to buy Kerston Hall. The place was mortgaged to its fullest value, and Julian took over the mortgages and foreclosed at the earliest opportunity.

When the foreclosure was threatened, Mrs Kerston asked Julian to call on her. He found her a sad-faced, white-haired old lady, with a disconcerting likeness to her son, and something reminiscent of him in her manner of speaking. She came to the point at once.

'I understand that this house is now practically yours, Mr Maltrey,' she said.

She cut him short as he began to protest.

'It is all the same,' she said, 'It will be yours within a few weeks. I have asked you to come and see me because I wish to warn you.'

'To warn me, madam!' Julian repeated blankly.

'Yes. My son hated you, and you hated him—no, do not contradict me, it is necessary that we should understand each other. You remember the day he died? He was conscious half an hour before the end, and he begged me not to allow this house to fall into your hands. He seemed to have a presentiment of what was going to happen. At the risk of offending you, Mr Maltrey, I must tell you that the idea of your living here was hateful to him.'

'I can well understand that,' Julian answered, 'and although I would do my utmost to humour the wishes of a dying man, I cannot allow them to alter my plans to the extent you seem to desire.'

'Mr Maltrey,' she said earnestly, 'I beg of you to sell this property the moment it becomes yours, and on no account to live here.'

Julian's natural obstinacy was aroused.

'Why shouldn't I?' he demanded bluntly.

Mrs Kerston lowered her voice. 'Because you will not be safe. Because my son swore that he would kill you if you ever made this house your home.'

'But—how can that be possible?' Julian asked, surprised and incredulous.

'You are not a superstitious man, I see,' she said, with a quiet little smile—Godfrey Kerston's smile. 'How he will do it is more than I can tell you. But he will! My son is a Kerston, and Kerstons do not break their word.'

I do not know what passed between them after that. I only know that Julian came away more firmly resolved than ever to make Kerston Hall his home. There must have been some kink in his nature which I had not even suspected until then. He hated Godfrey Kerston dead as vehemently as he had hated him living.

'It is the finest piece of revenge that a man ever planned,' he once said 'There was a time when the young squire used to twit the grocer's brat. The old order changes, and the grocer's brat will shortly be my lord of the manor, while the late squire's body is rotting in its coffin. Gad! I only hope he will see it all!'

'Shut up!' I said impatiently. 'What a beastly idea! It's a pretty mean triumph after all to crow over a dead man. Take care he doesn't keep his word!'

Julian laughed, and laid a hand on my shoulder.

'Old boy,' he said, 'you mustn't think badly of me. I'm less of a humbug than the average man, that's all. Why should I pretend to forgive Kerston because he's dead? He didn't think very kindly of me when he was dying. Besides, you, of all other men, haven't much cause to stand up for him.'

'I know,' I admitted; 'I couldn't stand him, and I don't pretend to love him now. But he's dead, and the least we can do is to forget him.'

In due course Kerston Hall, with its ring-park and half-dozen farms, passed into Julian Maltrey's possession. The village church was on the estate and close to the house, so that by looking out of almost any window on the west side, one could see the great stone sepulchre beneath which lay the vault where many generations of Kerstons slept.

I'll have them out of it,' Julian said, I'll have another burial ground consecrated.'

I remonstrated with him, and he laughed.

'They're too close to the house,' he said, 'and I don't like it. If I were to pay any attention to that woman's words I should never sleep at night. If Kerston could keep his word he wouldn't have far to come, eh?' He finished with a laugh, but there was a false note in it, and it set me wondering if Julian had not been affected by Mrs Kerston's words a lot more than he cared to admit.

In due course an army of workmen arrived at the Hall. They renovated the old place from cellar to tower. Panels, on which were portraits of dead and gone Kerstons, most of them reminiscent of the man we had known and hated, were removed. A well-known firm of upholsterers sent down van-loads of ugly, modem furniture, while Julian stood by and chuckled at each act of vandalism. A staff of servants invaded the house in place of those whose forbears had been on the estate for generations. Julian handled the new broom with an expert hand.

One morning he looked in at my flat in town and found me at breakfast. He was cheerful, almost hilarious.

'Any engagements?' he asked, after the usual salutations.

'Plenty,' said I.

'Well, scratch 'em. You're coming down to Kerston with me this morning, and as soon as the place is straight, we'll give a house-warming to just a few of the people we know who won't do us any harm with the county. By the way, I have discovered that young Kerston was rather keen on a girl who'll be a near neighbour of mine. Her people wouldn't let them marry for financial reasons. Do you know—I think of marrying her myself.'

'You're a devil!' I said, and I meant it.

He laughed and patted me on the shoulder.

'No,' he said, 'not a devil. Just your old friend Julian, whose worst fault is that he can't forgive an enemy, even if that enemy happens to be dead.' I shook myself free of him with a gesture of impatience, for he had jarred on me. But I went with him to Kerston all the same.

I was not comfortable at Kerston Hall, even in broad daylight. There were dark comers in every room where the sun could not penetrate; there were also noises, easy to explain, but not the less disquieting. It was a house of depression, in spite of new furniture and fresh paint. I had not been there an hour before I determined to leave as soon as possible.

Julian went everywhere with a smile on his lips, sometimes humming the snatch of a song; but often, when he thought I was not observing him, I saw his face turn grey and thoughtful, and knew that the wretched sensation of depression had affected him too.

That night, when we went up to dress for dinner, he came into my room to shave, and sat on my bed, chatting, until I was ready to go down, when he asked me to come to his room and wait until he had finished his toilet. We dined in solitary state in the great, lofty dining-room, with its huge fireplace still emblazoned with the Kerston arms, and the silent, mocking faces of nymphs and goddesses watching us from the high ceiling. We felt that we had no right to be there, that the house was not Julian's, although his money had bought it.

I do not think we exchanged more than a dozen words during that wretched meal. We had nothing to say that could be said within the hearing of the stolid servants who waited behind our chairs. When they left us to our wine, Julian began to talk feverishly. He told a funny story at which we both laughed merely for the sake of laughing, until the echoes silenced us with their sinister mocking.

Julian drained his glass and sprang to his feet.

'Come on!' he said, I'll play you a couple of hundred up. Bring the cigars in with you. I'll tell them to fetch some whisky.'

The billiard-room was just across the hall. Julian preceded me thither and turned on the shaded lights. 'We'll mark for ourselves,' he said; 'we shall be more comfortable.'

We both played wretchedly, although, as a rule, we were not mean performers with the cue. From outside we could hear the soft footfalls of servants hurrying to and fro, and from the dining-room the occasional clatter of a plate or the tinkle of glass and silver told us that they were clearing the table. Suddenly we heard voices from the open doorway of the dining-room.

Two of the servants seemed to be arguing over something. I heard Sprules, the butler, say very' distinctly, 'Well, I'll go and see.'

I was standing with my back to the door, placing my ball in baulk. At the opposite end of the table, Julian waited to see the effect of my shot, resting on his cue.

'Look outside and see what's wrong,' he said.

I nodded and went out, taking my cue with me. Turning a comer which brought me into the wide entrance-hall, I saw Sprules standing on the threshold, staring out into the night.

'What's the matter?' I asked.

He started as if he had been stung. 'I—I thought I heard the bell go,' he faltered.

'That's impossible,' I said. 'No bell rang. We should have heard it in the billiard-room.'

The man grinned sheepishly. 'That's true, sir,' he said. 'The bell didn't ring; but I had a feeling—leastways, sir, I thought there was someone outside the door that wanted to come in.'

As he spoke a faint noise reached my ears. It was infinitely queer.

'You've been drinking,' I said hurriedly, more for the sake of speaking than because I believed my charge to be well founded.

'Not a drop, sir,' the man replied indignantly.

I shrugged my shoulders and tried to speak calmly. 'What is this noise?' I asked. 'And where does it come from?'

'Ah! So you can hear it too, sir! I noticed it just as I opened the door, but it's quiet again now.'

I pulled myself together with an effort, and spoke impatiently.

'Oh, come inside and close the door, there's a fearful draught.'

And with that I returned to the billiard-room.

I found Julian standing just where I had left him; I do not think that he had moved during my absence from the room.

'Well,' he asked, 'what's wrong?'

'Oh, nothing,' I answered shortly. 'Sprules thought he heard someone at the door, and of course there was no one there.'

'Then Sprules will take a month's notice,' Julian said grimly. 'I bar keeping imaginative servants. My nerves are none too good as it is, so - Hullo! What on earth '

He broke off and glanced covertly at me. Our eyes met across the table under the shaded lights.

'Can you hear anything?' he asked.

'Yes,' I said. 'I noticed it just now out in the hall, and I can hear it again now.'

'Well,' he snapped, 'it's nothing to laugh at!'

'I didn't laugh,' I answered. 'It was you. You don't know what you are doing tonight.'

'It was some sound in the wall, I expect,' Julian said, taking hurried, nervous glances to right and left. 'Old houses are full of such sounds, especially at night.'

He glanced at me as if he wished me to agree with him, and suddenly I saw his jaw drop, and his eyes widen and bulge.

'For God's sake, man, don't look at me like that!' he cried. 'Dicky, old boy, what's the matter?'

'Nothing,' I answered hoarsely. But I, too, was afraid—afraid of myself. As I watched Julian, a sudden fierce desire possessed me to take his throat between my hands and squeeze, squeeze, squeeze until my fingers met! He must have read the thought in my eyes, for his face betrayed a terror such as I had never seen before. The next moment I loved Julian again as much as ever, and stood in wonder at myself for the inexplicable desire which had passed over me. I walked round the table, and patted him on the back.

'Buck up, old man!' I said. 'Our nerves are out of order. Let's chuck playing and turn in.'

He was trembling as if he had been suddenly smitten with ague.

'Dicky,' he said, 'you looked like a devil just now!'

'Nonsense!' I laughed.

Was it only the echo of my laugh that rumbled discordantly through the room? Surely my lips could never have uttered so sinister a sound! I slept badly that night, and longed for the black rectangle of the window' to turn grey. Once in the night I was again possessed by the insane desire to seize Julian by the throat, and squeeze the life out of his body. It was then that I seemed to feel that something was in the room, and vague and subtle as the feeling was, I felt it was something overpoweringly horrible. For the first time in my life I drew the bedclothes over my head for fear.

After breakfast next morning Julian and I spent a long day on the estate. It did us good, I think; but all the while we were thinking of the coming night, and dreading it. Dinner was laid that evening in a smaller room, and we found it more comfortable and cheerful than the great dining-room. Sprules had not waited to be asked to leave. He and one of the footmen had given notice after lunch, and I think Julian was prepared for others to follow their example.

Julian had turned a small morning-room into a 'den'. It was by far the pleasantest room in the house, comfortably furnished, and full of little knick-knacks, reminiscent of old times. The dictionaries he had used at school were in a bookcase which he had brought down with him from Oxford; shields emblazoned with our college arms hung over the mantelshelf; a cricket-bag stood upright in a comer, and I fancy Julian had placed it there because it was comfortable to look at, and reminiscent of halcyon days.

We adjourned there after dinner, and found it much more to our mood than the billiard-room. A grey Persian cat lay curled up on the hearth-rug fast asleep. The cat had once been owned by Godfrey Kerston, and it was the only remaining thing in the house that had belonged to him. The animal refused to leave its old haunts, and rather than kill it, Julian let it stay.

Should I ever forget that last evening we spent together, even if my life were allowed to run its natural course? Each was intent upon cheering the other, and we talked of old times, and little jokes and stories which had been half forgotten returned to us. Then It came in, and the laughter died away from our lips.

Julian got upon his legs, frowning and clenching his hands.

'That infernal noise again!' he muttered. 'What can it be?'

There was silence for nearly a minute, and then I heard myself speak.

'Kerston!' I muttered, without knowing why, 'Kerston!'

Julian turned his dull eyes on me. 'What made you say that?' he cried.

'I don't know,' I answered lamely. 'Good God, man, look at that cat!'

The cat had woken up, stretched, purred, and licked its paws. Then it had risen silently, and was moving stealthily towards the middle of the room, purring a welcome to someone we could not see Presently it stopped and arched its back, and began to move its head up and down with a peculiar sideward motion. It was as if the animal were rubbing its head against the legs of some invisible person. We watched it in icy horror.

Julian bent down towards the fireplace, reached out an arm, and groped with his hand until his fingers encountered the poker. All the while he was watching the cat. There was a swift movement and a crash. The poker missed the cat by a hair's-breadth, and the startled animal fled under a chair. Julian crossed the room and picked up the poker, laughing uneasily.

'Dicky,' he said, 'there's something wrong with both of us. Our nerves'

It's not our nerves,' I cried, it's this infernal house! Let's clear out! There's something we can't see walking about the place day and night! We can both feel it! It's Kerston!'

There was fear in Julian's eyes, but he set his lips and squared his shoulders.

'Then Kerston may go back to the devil!' he cried. 'If it is he, I'm not going to allow him to turn me out. I didn't care a snap of my fingers for him living, and I care as little for him dead!'

'Julian,' I said, 'if you don't go, I must! No, no, old man, it's not because I'm afraid, but every time he comes into the room I feel'

'Yes,' said Julian.

But I never finished the sentence. I wanted to tell Julian of my mad fits of desire to kill him when I felt the influence of the Something that disturbed our peace. But I hadn't the heart to say it, and remained silent. Julian lit a cigar and poured out a drink.

'Look here,' he said, 'you and I are going to see this thing through. If we shirk, it's a triumph for—him. But I'm going to leave nothing to chance. I'm not going to sleep alone in this place, for the present at any rate. You'll have to sleep in my room.'

I demurred, but he insisted. When our wills crossed it was generally Julian who got his way. He rang the bell and gave orders for another bed to be brought into his room.

I dropped off to sleep early, secure in the knowledge that Julian was only a yard or so away.

It must have been about two o'clock when I woke. The room was dark, but the moon-light found tiny chinks in the blind, and made the furniture faintly visible. I was drenched with perspiration, and a horror, such as I had never felt before, clutched at my throat. I tried to cry out and could not. It was like a hideous nightmare, but all the while I was awake and conscious. I could hear Julian's breathing, deep and regular, and one of those dreadful spasms of hatred for my best friend stole over me again. Stole, did I say? In a minute it had possessed me. It overcame my terror, it caused me to struggle out of bed and take a step in the direction of Julian's prostrate body. Step by step, and each step a separate agony, I remember moving across the floor over the little white patches of moonlight. All the while I tried to reason with myself, to combat with the evil thing that had mastered my body.

I heard someone laugh, and I was not frightened, although I knew that it could not be Julian. Perhaps it was I who laughed. I do not know.

The darkness became a deep red mist, and the stillness was broken by a stifled cry, a worrying growl, a tempestuous thrashing of limbs against bedclothes. My mind is almost a blank. I do not remember. Ah, God, how horrible it was!

Suddenly I found myself staring down at Julian. His face was black, there were multi-coloured marks upon his throat, he lay very still. He was dead! I did not believe it at first, nor that my hands had done this thing. I called him by name, but he did not answer. Then, as I knelt beside him, sobbing like a child, his valet, who had heard his cries, burst into the room. The man stated at the inquest that it was a long time before anyone could convince me that Julian was really dead.

I have written a true account of the circumstances connected with Julian's death, and the writing of it has done me good. I am very tired, and I think I shall sleep a little. My consolation is that Julian knows it was Kerston's will and not mine that killed him—that on that dreadful night I was governed by something stronger than mine own self. I do not know why Kerston's soul was allowed to dominate mine; but very soon this mystery, and many others, will be made clear to me. And this too I know, that tomorrow they will hang an innocent man—a man whose soul is clean, if his hands are red.

And this Julian understands, and he will be my witness before the Great Tribunal.

Someone in the Room

For or several reasons I believe Mrs Fairchild's story, but it may suffice if I name only two. The first and least is that I think her to be incapable of inventing anything on a more ambitious scale than those excuses of which, I gather, her creditors are already beginning to tire. The last and greatest is that Mrs Fairchild hates having to believe her own story, and quite plainly tries not to believe it. When she can be made to tell it—which is not often, and only under pressure from those whose good graces she wishes to preserve—she tries to interpolate a certain facetiousness which falls rather flat.

I have heard tales told by well-meaning folk who wish it to be believed that they have had experiences of the supernatural. They want so desperately to believe in, and convince others of, the survival of the spirit after death, that one feels them pathetically trying to believe their own well-intended inventions. In such matters knowledge is not always for the seekers, for Mrs Fairchild is certainly not of this school. I know her to be terrified of death, not because she dreads the thought of destruction but because she dreads the thought of survival. For her, the belief that she may have to expiate her unpicturesque sins in some terribly mixed state of society in which she may not be considered quite a lady, is a creed without comfort.

Mrs Fairchild, after some early struggles, had succeeded in ousting from her mind all those thoughts engendered by a conventionally religious upbringing, which are so uncomfortable to those who make it their only business to have a good time. In this one aim and object she had succeeded to admiration, although, having married Michael Fairchild in his palmy days, she had the chagrin of seeing the bulk of his fortune fall through the shafts of some out-worked mines in South Wales.

After that she became a sort of professional poor relation. She and Michael had a stuffy little flat squeezed just inside the postal district of Mayfair whither they retired when through ill-luck or temporary mismanagement there was no other roof to cover them; but for ten months of the year they contrived to live in other people's country houses, on other people's yachts, in other people's Continental villas—anywhere, in fact, where there was amusing company and good board and lodging to be had for nothing. The experience which befell Mrs Fairchild, which I am about to relate, happened some two years ago. It was in the autumn and the Fairchilds were temporarily separated while Michael joined a bachelor shooting party in a Devon farmhouse. They had both been staying with Joan Fairchild's uncle and aunt right down in the toe of Cornwall, and Joan stayed on under the avuncular roof until it was such time as she was due to join Michael at a country house near Liskeard.

On the day when she was due to depart Joan Fairchild crowned a somewhat inauspicious visit by missing the only train which could convey her to her destination by nightfall. She returned crestfallen to meet an aunt who shared her disappointment but without loss of sympathy. The house was due to fill again on the morrow, and if dear Joan didn't go when she said she was going there was no saying when the broadest hints would dislodge her.

If her aunt were anxious to speed the parting guest Joan Fairchild was equally anxious to be sped. She had some of the pagan superstitions of the age, and stigmatized the house she was trying to leave as Unlucky. For the last four days she had been made painfully aware that bridge is a game of aces and kings and that skill is of no avail against the kind of brute force which scores hundreds for aces above the line. The sooner she was gone the better. Moreover her absence from the other end would leave an odd number, and she was particularly anxious not to inconvenience the Paley-Thomtons, who had just taken a villa for the season at Cannes.

Her aunt solved the problem by consulting road-maps, speculating as to how long she could comfortably forgo the services of Cox the chauffeur and the use of her limousine, and by bribing Cox with the promise of a day's holiday some time during the following week. Cox looked doubtfully at a line of country on which first-class roads were conspicuously absent and contour lines extremely frequent and close together, but at last he said that he 'reckoned he could do it'. His task was to deposit Joan Fairchild safely in the neighbourhood of Liskeard in time for dinner, and return home by midnight. So it ended in Joan being lent Cox and the limousine and departing hastily, leaving her aunt moodily to reflect that relatives were an error on the part of Providence, and poor relatives a positive solecism.

Joan Fairchild travelled without a maid, and borrowed assistance from her hostesses. She had for company on the journey only a curtailed back view of Cox seen through the glass, his green-clad shoulders, his red ears and neck, and the top of his back-tilted cap which adhered to his head like a rakish halo. She had schemed to escape altogether without tipping him; and now she wondered if a pound note would evoke that dumb insolence to which, from other people's servants, she was becoming used. Probably he would linger to take refreshment at the Paley-Thorntons' and the over-fed, over-paid beast might easily warn the servants' hall against devoting too much attention to the comfort of an unprofitable guest. Since she had begun to live partly on charity and partly by her wits she had come to observe in servants certain uncomfortable penetrative faculties.

As a defensive measure she began to complain against the slowness of his driving. The roads were no better than mazes of lanes and the hills were mountainous. Cox was soon behind on his self-compiled timetable, and before half the distance had been covered it was plain that Joan Fairchild would not arrive in time for dinner. The goaded Cox courted disaster by trying to recover lost time, and it was just as dusk was falling that the accident happened.

They were descending a corkscrew hill with occasional gradients which flung Joan Fairchild forward in her seat, when Cox took a bend at a pace which swung him on to the wrong side, to meet a Ford lorry which was toiling up, boiling water spouting from its radiator as from a geyser. Cox missed the lorry by inches and by a miracle, and Joan Fairchild bounced like a die in a dice-box. She was hardly back on the seat before she was shaken off it again. The car heaved itself on to roadside grass, plunged forward leaning at an angle, then stopped with a crash and a jolt.

When she had recovered herself sufficiently to climb out she found Cox ruefully regarding a ripped front tyre, the stump of a tree and a broken front axle. Cox's pallor of face was evidence that he thought things might have been worse. In a few well-chosen words he told her the extent of the damage. What Joan Fairchild found to say to Cox and what Cox replied to Joan Fairchild are not on record. We are only told that Cox was quite impudent about it, nor was he very helpful when Joan asked him what he was going to do. Moreover he did not seem to know where he was, save that he was on the right road, nor the nearest place whence assistance could be obtained.

So far as Joan Fairchild had been able to notice, they had been passing through a tract of wild and desolate country, scarred with the shafts of deserted tin mines. Houses were few, but it happened that she had seen one on the top of the hill which they had half descended. It looked to her like a farmhouse. So she sent Cox up to inquire their whereabouts and the locality of the nearest garage and post-office.

Cox was absent about a quarter of an hour and returned with a long face,

'I've seen the lady and gentleman, ma'am, and they say that the nearest garage and post-office is five miles on.'

'Oh, they're a lady and gentleman, are they?' said Joan hopefully.

'You'd be a better judge about that than me, ma'am,' said Cox guardedly.

'Are they on the telephone?'

'No, ma'am; I asked.'

'Well, what did they think we'd better do?'

'They said a car might be coming along the road that would take a message.'

'But suppose one doesn't?'

'I don't know, ma'am.'

'And even if we get help, I suppose it will be impossible to get on the road again to-night.'

'That's true, ma'am,' said Cox equably. After all, he was not due to stay at the Paley-Thorntons'.

Joan Fairchild stamped her foot for sheer irritation.

'Well, the best thing you can do,' she said, 'is to walk to this wretched village, tell the garage people about the car, and try and get a hired one to take me on.'

Cox presented her with a blank stare.

'What, me walk five miles!' he said. He bent and caressed one of his calves. 'Beg pardon, ma'am, but I got a packet here in the War.'

'Well, we can't be here all night,' said Joan Fairchild with that air of finality which she always used in dismissing unpleasant possibilities.

The dialogue was interrupted by the sound of footfalls descending the hill. A male figure hove in sight, and Cox remarked sotto voce that here was the gentleman from the house on the top. A closer inspection revealed to Joan Fairchild a tall, rugged man in early middle-life, clad in old pale-grey tweeds which, she said, made him look like a dirty sheep. When he drew near he pulled off his cap and addressed Joan Fairchild in accents in which there were distinct traces of the Midlands.

'I'm afraid you're in trouble,' he said. 'Mrs Fifield and I have been talking it over and we're both afraid you may not be able to get on to-night. If you can't, we'd be pleased to give you a room. We both know what it's like to be stranded.'

Joan Fairchild gushed, and considered while she gushed. Mrs Fifield was evidently the wife of this good Samaritan, and she realised that, while they were not 'her kind of people' it would be impossible to offer them money. On the other hand she would feel morally compelled to send them a more or less expensive present, and she would have to endure their company which, instinct told her, would be no small penance.

'Oh, not at all,' said the Samaritan in reply to the gush, it would be a hard world if we couldn't help each other. Besides, we don't get much company. There's a nice spare room and some hot supper.'

'There's my chauffeur,' said Joan Fairchild doubtfully.

'He can have the second spare room, and I shouldn't be surprised if we can find a bit of hot supper for him too.'

Cox was plainly very much in favour of the proposal and remarked in a low tone that he didn't see much hopes of getting any further that evening. Joan reflected that even if she were able to get on the road again in another car she could only hope to arrive at the Paley-Thorntons' at some hour which would not enhance her popularity. Besides, she found herself already tired and hungry. So, with a graciousness and many expressions of thanks which constituted a fine piece of acting, she accepted the invitation.

The house was one of nine or ten rooms, built of Cornish granite and inexpressibly hideous on the outside. The interior was not much more prepossessing, save that oil lamps were burning, and a good fire blazed in the grate of a hybrid apartment which was neither dining-room nor drawing-room. Here Joan Fairchild was greeted by her prospective hostess, a faded woman of about forty who wore a tweed skirt and a dove-grey woollen jumper.

Mrs Fifield's greeting was at once hearty and sympathetic, but the heartiness soon died away, as if a false note had been struck in a house of depression. Joan Fairchild looked around the room and shuddered. It was a museum of all those decorative horrors which an educated taste had taught her to despise. The fireplace was small and bordered by hideous green tiles, the grate narrow, shallow, and plainly constructed for the purpose of economizing in coals. The furniture belonged to the worst phase of the Victorian era, and the pictures were mostly depressing engravings and framed photographs of people who bore the authentic stamp of such relatives and friends as she would have expected the Fifields to possess.

Much hospitality pushed Joan near the fire, then thrust her from one chair into another which was alleged to be more comfortable, then conducted her upstairs into the conjugal chamber for the removal of her hat. Then followed a leaden half-hour before the fire, during which time the Fifields and their visitor tried vainly to find some common ground on which to meet and talk. Cox, sitting before the kitchen fire, was not faring much better with the one maid of the establishment, a taciturn Cornish girl who belonged to some eccentric religious sect, and believed that the stranger had been sent to her so that he could be saved. He resisted salvation with some energy and even lapsed further by cursing his temporary mistress under his breath. He regretted his eagerness to accept the invitation, and devoutly wished that he had walked the five miles despite the 'packet' in his leg.

Meanwhile Joan Fairchild smothered yawns, and tried to appear at least polite. She had none of the picnic instinct, and no sense of humour. Nor had she, with any innocent meaning, that golden attribute of the Apostle Paul. Her world consisted of the sort of people she cared to know, and of servants. She was aware of other people existing, but had never dreamed of being forced to meet them on terms of equality and had not the vaguest idea how to talk to them. She sat on with the miserable conviction that all the funny stories which she had heard about the middle-middle and lower-middle classes must be true.

But she tried hard to hide her snobbery, without the least suspicion that she was a snob. She told herself that if they had been bright and amusing after their own fashion she could have suffered them more or less gladly; but they were about as heavy and about as interesting as two great slabs of suet pudding.

This, she thought, might be partly due to the fact of their having recently endured trouble. Fifield wore a black tie and a diamond of crepe had been sewn on to one of his sleeves. The air was heavy with melancholy, and the house itself was like some monstrous figure of grief brooding alone on the hill-top In the course of desultory talk Joan Fairchild learned that her host had been 'in business' and had been compelled to retire some two years since on account of his nerves. That he suffered from some nervous disorder was plain, for often when he talked his lower jaw gave a sidelong twitch. He spent his enforced retirement in rearing chickens and tame rabbits, on which subjects he showed symptoms of being prepared to converse.

The guest uttered an inaudible sigh of relief when at last the taciturn maid came in to lay the table, but her heart sank when a dish of stewed rabbit appeared. She had not tasted it since she was in the schoolroom, and remembered hating it even then. The possibility that it was one of the tame rabbits, and the unlikely but unwholesome thought that it might have died a natural death, did not help her appetite when she sat down at the table. She toyed with her food and talked on any and every subject that entered her head in an effort to conceal the fact that she was not eating. There followed some tinned fruit which she was able to swallow, but on sipping from her glass she wondered why poets of the breezy, swashbuckling school wrote songs in praise of cider.

'I think you'll find your room comfortable,' Mrs Fifield assured her. 'It hasn't been slept in for six months, but we have kept it well aired and there has been a fire in it once a week since the cold, damp weather started. We have very few people to stay with us.'

The last statement did not strain Mrs Fairchild's credulity. Whatever gratitude she may have had in her composition, and it was not her most salient characteristic, had been choked out of her by boredom and a desolating sensation of strangeness. The world was only for herself and the people who amused her. That these strangers had gone to some inconvenience to feed, house and attempt to entertain her was a matter which counted for nothing to a lady who had made a fine art of selfishness.

She sat on, wondering how soon common decency would allow her to shed a hint about going to bed. There were symptoms of the rabbit-chicken conversation beginning over again. Normally she hated her own company and would not have dreamed of retiring for hours; but anything was preferable to the company of these two incredible bores.

At last Mrs Fifield gave her the desired opportunity.

'You look tired,' she said. 'Wouldn't you like to go to your room?'

Joan Fairchild exhibited a smile which was almost vivacious.

'Well, really,' she said, 'if you don't mind I almost think I should.'

'We're early birds ourselves,' remarked Mrs Fifield. 'And you've come a long way, haven't you?'

She said good night to her host, and Mrs Fifield conducted her upstairs with a lighted candle and threw open the door of a medium-sized room, facing south. The furniture and pictures were such as Joan Fairchild had told herself to expect; but the bed looked comfortable, and when the light was out she need not notice her surroundings.

Mrs Fifield cast a deprecating glance at the hearth. A fire had been laid and lit, but only the paper had burned.

'There now,' she said, 'I told that girl to light a fire, and she hasn't stayed to watch if it burned up.'

Joan Fairchild smothered a yawn.

'Never mind, thank you,' she said, i shall be going straight to bed. Good night, Mrs Fifield, and thank you so much.'

The door closed, but she was not left long to herself. Mrs Fifield returned and tapped at her door at least half a dozen times, bringing little things supposed to minister to her comfort. But the well-intentioned persecution ceased at last, and Joan Fairchild unlocked one of her trunks and took out such articles of toilet as she required for the night. By the time she had blown out her candle and got into bed all members of the household were upstairs and the house was still.

She says that she slept almost at once, but fitfully, and whenever she half woke she heard a kind of whispering, such as many people imagine they hear when they lie in a state of semi-consciousness. A voice which she imagined was produced by her own sub-consciousness proceeded to count in a whisper and very slowly and carefully. 'One, two, three four, five, six,' it said. It never got further than six, and then began over again.

After one of these periods Joan Fairchild woke completely, but she lay still, and smiled at her own aberration. Why had she repeatedly counted up to six? What had she been dreaming? Probably she had been playing in her sleep some absurd hand at bridge, and had been counting the cards still unplayed in a certain suit. What deplorable luck she had been having lately! That awful game consisting of three hands; three down doubled on quite a reasonable spade call, and then two little slams in no trumps made by the other side. But it couldn't go on like that. At the Paley-Thorntons' . . . And, without realizing it, she was half-asleep again.

'One, two, three, four, five, six'

She woke again, this time violently. The whispered voice had seemed not to proceed from her own brain. It seemed to her that she had actually heard it from outside, from somewhere in the room. The breath in her nostrils turned cold. She turned over in bed and looked around her fearfully.

The moon had climbed the sky outside and lit up the room. A long flag of silvery light from the window lay unfurled upon the floor and reached to the washstand opposite. Even the shadows were not impenetrable, and Joan Fairchild, examining every dim curtain of shade, let her breath go freely at seeing no suspicious shape. Her imagination had played a trick upon her and she was quite alone.

Then something on the washstand caught her attention. It was a stray moonbeam which had focused there on some particular object. She lay wondering what it was, but without sufficient curiosity to get up and see; and after a while discovered that it was the tooth glass which she had used and set down there before retiring. She turned over and tried once more to sleep.

This time she tried in vain. Her nerves had been more highly strained than she had supposed. She heard stealthy movements about her in the room, the furniture began to creak and rap, and all the half-forgotten bogies of her childhood returned to torment her.

Quite uselessly she asked herself what she had to fear. It was all nerves, all imagination. Something seemed to be moving over by the washstand.

There were little senseless noises like the tinkling of glass and the clink of toilet-ware. But she wouldn't look. What was the use of looking when it was all 'nerves' and there was nothing to see?

'One, two, three'

She turned over with a muffled scream, lashing the bedclothes with her limbs. She had not whispered that, nor had she imagined it. Somebody in the room was whispering aloud; somebody by the washstand.

She forced herself to look, and there was nothing. Only the moonbeam was now dancing, moving up and down and to and fro, as if somebody were toying and hesitating with the glass. So it wasn't the glass after all . . .

And then her heart stopped, and for so long that she felt it would never start again. It was the glass, and apparently it was moving in the air of its own volition. Then she saw the moonbeam dim and something like the shadow of a hand encircled the tumbler.

Joan Fairchild sat up in bed and pressed two hands to a heart which rioted now like some caged and frenzied beast. A shadow beside the washstand grew out of nothing, and increased in visibility and substance, 'I'm not mad and I'm not dreaming,' she thought in her misery. 'Then, oh God! what is it?'

The tooth glass was replaced on the tiled washstand with an audible clink. She was now quite definitely not alone in the room. An elderly, grey-bearded man in shabby grey pyjamas had set it down, and he took up a medicine bottle which he leaned very carefully over the rim.

'One, two, three, four, five, six.'

She could not cry out nor take her eyes from him, but he turned and fixed her with a haggard gaze of agony, as if to make sure that she was following his movements. And in the midst of the tortures of her mind Joan Fairchild knew that her creed of materialism was all a pricked bubble, that the dead survive, that the thing with the glass in its hand was something not of this world but yet a living and conscious entity.

She knew that he was in that state which the Churchmen call Hell, that he was vile and odious and suffering, that he had done in life the thing that he was about to do again. He put the glass to his lips, threw back his head and drank, set down the glass, and, to the wretched woman's indescribable panic, he advanced towards her.

He had not taken two steps when his eyes rolled, he clutched at his throat, swayed, writhed and plunged forward, sinking on to his knees as he clutched at the bedclothes, and burying his face in the eiderdown.

Then, for a moment, Joan Fairchild went mad. She clawed at the Horror, touching nothing. She caught at her pillow and lashed and lashed at the bowed head. Then it slipped off the edge of the bed and she saw on the floor a shapeless mass slowly melting like mist before the sun.

I don't know what clothes she put on before letting herself out of the house. She says that she ran down the hill barefooted to the car, that she dressed inside in the dark, and that she cried and moaned all the while. But some time before dawn she fell asleep for she was awakened by Cox in broad daylight.

'Good morning, ma'am,' he said, trying to conceal his surprise. 'The people up at the 'ouse said you must have got up very early and gone out, and I guessed you must have gone down to the car. Well, I've just stopped a man in a Morris up the road, and he's promised to send help along from the nearest place.'

Joan Fairchild nodded without interest.

'Go back and get my luggage,' she said, 'and bring it down here. I can't go back. Tell the people at the house anything—anything you like, I'm not going back there.'

Cox eyed her with respectful solicitude.

'Beg pardon, ma'am, but is anything the matter?'

'No, nothing,' she answered. 'Don't worry me.'

'It's that 'ouse give you the creeps, ma'am,' said Cox. i don't wonder, for it fair gave 'em to me. They 'ad one suicide there six months ago, and I'm not surprised, although'

'They—what?' Joan Fairchild cried.

'Suicide, ma'am. Mrs Fifield's father it was. Their servant was telling me all about it. He poisoned himself one night. He was a pretty bad lot from what she told me. The police were going to arrest him for something nasty. I don't know for what, because she either didn't know or wouldn't tell me. But'

'Oh, stop!' cried Joan Fairchild, and thrust her fingers into her ears.

Cox regarded her in dismay.

'I beg pardon, ma'am. I didn't mean to upset you at all. Do you feel ill, ma'am?'

Joan Fairchild made a spasmodic movement and thrust her face into the palms of her hands.

'Yes,' she cried hysterically, i feel ill—I feel ill!'

And, with her face buried, she began to rock herself to and fro.

The Shadowy Escort

Almost everybody has at one time or another wanted to write a detective story, but, for the greater well-being of publishers and publishers' readers, not everybody has tried. Among those who have, with varying degrees of success, must be numbered a lot of men and women who would not have attempted to enter the realm of letters by any other frontier. Detective fiction has a fascination for nearly every type of mind. Thus it may happen that the butcher's boy cannot bring himself to deliver the meat until he has read the explanation of what really did happen in Chapter Six, and the Cabinet Minister, also immersed in another copy of the same work, forgets to protest because his dinner is late.

This is due to the age-old, natural, human love of a puzzle; and the ambition to create a puzzle of one's own, instead of merely trying to solve other peoples', is a natural after-growth.

Serrald had read detective fiction for years as a mental relaxation. When he dined out he talked about the Russian School and the influence of the Arthurian Legend upon our early poets; when he got home he went on reading The Mystery of Bloodshot Grange. This he regarded as a secret vice, and did not own to it until he discovered that many of his intellectual friends, who also should have known better, made similar concessions to their lower natures.

Serrald was a man in the middle thirties who liked to pose as an intellectual. He was employed in one of the higher branches of the Civil Service, and had been immune from any other service during the early years of the War. But when the newspapers had invented 'Cuthbert', and printed rude remarks about Government Rabbit Warrens, he had joined the Army as a private, and later received a commission after several months' service in France. Apparently he had done very well in the Army, but he rarely spoke about those days. The War had been too vulgar a brawl for a young man with a taste for intellectualism.

It was some years after the War that Serrald confided to his friend Masters his intention of writing a detective novel. He said that it might be better fun than continuing to read them, and that there must be a lot of fun to be had in laying false clues and finding for them sound and logical reasons for being included in the tale.

'I mean,' he added, 'to write a perfectly insoluble mystery story—insoluble, that is, until the reader has reached the last page.'

Masters smiled at this modest ambition.

'Any ideas?' he asked.

'Oh, yes. My murder is going to be an act of omission, not of commission. The murderer turns out to be only a murderer in the sense that he has found his victim in a predicament in which death must supervene if he refuses help—and he just refuses help and leaves him to die. There is another strong criminal interest in the story, but before I can get on with it I've got to invent something new in the way of ciphers. I want a cipher that doesn't look like a cipher. It must, of course, be very difficult to solve and be very innocent in appearance, so that anybody finding it would scarcely guess that it conveyed a message at all.'

Masters considered.

'Short or long messages?' he asked.

'Oh, short would do. Just something by which criminals could warn each other of danger, and make appointments, and all that.'

'I'll have a good think,' said Masters, 'and tell you if anything occurs to me.'

Two evenings later he came round to Serrald's rooms, 'I've got your cipher,' he said, with the smile of one who anticipates praise.

'Oh? Got the key written down?'

'No. It hasn't to be written down. That's the beauty of it. It can be memorized in exactly one second. And nobody—except, of course, the super-human detective you intend to create—could possibly guess that it was a cipher. I think I'll take ten per cent commission on what you get out of your book.'

'We'll see,' said Serrald smiling.

'All right. Well, when one of your villains wants to communicate with another villain he just sends him a pack of cards. Or perhaps cards out of two or three packs. It depends on the length of the message required. And, of course, other cards might be added after the message was complete in order to ally suspicion in the event of the package going astray.'

'I don't quite follow you.'

'Well, my dear chap, there are twenty-six letters in the alphabet, and fifty-two cards to a pack. You take them in the order of their value at auction bridge. Thus the Ace of Spades is A, and the Two of Hearts is Z. Then we start again and the Ace of Diamonds becomes A and the Two of Clubs Z. That gives you two of every letter in one pack of cards.

'When one of your villains wants to tell another to "Beware" he sends him a pack of cards with the cipher ones at the top, in the order in which he will slide them off the pack. If the word were "Beware" the top card would be the King of Spades, then would come the Ten, W would be the Five of Hearts, A the Ace of Spades—or Diamonds if you like'

'By Jove!' Serrald exclaimed in genuine admiration.

'And the best of it is that the man who receives the message can instantly destroy all traces of it by merely shuffling the cards. Similarly anybody who guessed that the cards meant something, and started monkeying with them, would spoil his own chance of deciphering the message as soon as he altered their sequence.'

Serrald nodded. 'That's quite a brilliant idea. You go from the top to the bottom of the Spades, and then from the top to the bottom of the Hearts, and that gives you the alphabet. Ace of Hearts would be the fourteenth letter, which is—er—N'

'Ace of Hearts and Ace of Clubs are both N's. You go straight down the Spades and then straight down the Hearts. That's one alphabet of letters. Then straight down the Diamonds and straight down the Clubs, and that's another. Of course, one pack of cards wouldn't go far if you wanted a longish message, because so many letters get duplicated so quickly. Your crooks would have to keep about ten packs of cards each, all of the same pattern, to send longish messages to each other without anybody who might casually see the cards suspecting there was a code.'

i've got it. Well, I've got stacks of cards here, red-backs, and blue-backs, all of the same pattern. I get them from the stores for bridge, you know, and about twice a year I send the old ones to a hospital. I'll get some out and spell you a message to see if I've got it right.'

He went to a drawer and pulled out fourteen or fifteen discarded packs which had been thrust back into their cardboard cases, and poured them all out upon the table, pack after pack, after which he began stirring the heap with his hands.

'Let's see,' he said, 'I'll pull out a few cards at random first of all, and see if I can remember which letters they represent. Here's the Two of Diamonds. What's that?'

'M,' said Masters. 'Two of Spades and Two of Diamonds are both M's. What's that you've got there now? King of Hearts? That's O. Ace of Hearts is an N. Four of Diamonds—that's K. Hullo, we've fluked a word already—Monk. Carry on. That's an L. Ace of Spades—that's an A. Not too quick. 'Nother Ace of Hearts is another N. Knave of Diamonds D. That's funny. Two words come out running—Monk and Land.'

Serrald pushed the cards away from him with an impatient gesture. He had turned suddenly pale and a cold sweat shone on his face.

'Yes,' he said, quickly and unsteadily, 'I understand it now. It's—yes, it's devilish clever. Have a drink, will you? No, I don't want to know any more about it. A child could understand it once he'd been told. Yes, it's devilish clever—devilish clever.'

Masters stared at his friend with sudden anxiety and a kind of dismay.

'You're feeling all right, aren't you?' he asked.

'Oh, quite. Quite all right. Why? Whisky for you?'

'Thanks. But you do look a bit green, you know. I thought perhaps'

'What?'

'Oh, nothing. Because the cards you pulled out at random happen to spell two words, it looked as if you thought there might be something uncanny about it. They're not very significant words, and I don't see how they could be tacked together to start a sentence. I invented the code last night and amused myself in the same way, to help me memorize it, by drawing cards at random and seeing if they'd form words. But I never got anything of more than four letters. Some promising starts at ambitious words, and then gibberish.'

Serrald had risen. He poured out two drinks and swallowed his own quickly.

'I'm a bit tired,' he said, 'that's all.' He kept his face averted. 'Of course, one might go on picking out cards at random for ever without finding sequences which would spell words. That's what makes it so—so excellent as a cipher, when one knows the key. It's a really excellent idea of yours. I shall certainly use it in my story.'

The two men met frequently, and it was natural after that for Masters, who felt almost a proprietary interest in the detective romance, to inquire after its progress. But, like that of so many would-be authors, Serrald's enthusiasm seemed to have set sharp upon its rising. He explained that he wasn't well, and that it was no use making a start on the job until he felt fit to tackle it properly. Indeed, he had taken to looking ill, and to drinking a great deal more than was good for a man with a nervous temperament. Masters regarded him with the dispassionate pity of one who sees disaster looming ahead for another—a disaster for which the spectator is neither responsible nor able to avert.

'That chap's in for some sort of a breakdown,' he thought.

About a month later Masters had occasion one evening to go and pay Serrald a call. Serrald lived on the second floor of a large 'apartments' house in Bloomsbury, of which the street door was always kept open until late at night. He mounted the dark stairs and had reached the second-floor landing, when he became aware of a figure moving away from the door of Serrald's sitting-room. Masters made way for it with a muttered word of apology and watched it descend half a dozen of the stairs before he turned and tapped at Serrald's door. Something quite inexplicable in the sight of the figure that had passed him filled him with a kind of cold dismay.

The sound of his knuckles on the door provoked loud and startled exclamation from within.

'Who's there? Who 's there?'

'It's only I,' said Masters, and pushed open the door.

Inside the room Serrald, wild-haired and wild-eyed, had swung round in his chair to face the door. He was sitting before a large central table on which was piled a great muddled heap of playing cards.

'Hullo,' said Masters in a level and pleasant voice. 'Hope you don't mind my butting in. I know I didn't drive your other visitor away, because he'd started to go before I got here.'

Lines grew on Serrald's white face. For a moment he showed the whites of his eyes.

'My other visitor?' he repeated.

'Army chap.'

Serrald drew breath noisily.

'Army chap—how do you know?'

'Wore the uniform of an officer. Sorry, I expect I made a mistake.

Thought he was moving away from your door.'

'Officers don't wear uniform in peace time, except when they're on duty,' Serrald said thickly.

'I know. But this one was wearing his. I dare say he's a London Terrier just come from his drill-hall.'

Serrald gulped.

'What was he like?' he faltered. 'Tall?'

'Tall, yes, and broad. Couldn't see much what he was like apart from that. But he looked— well, the general impression I got was—that his uniform wasn't exactly smart enough for the parade ground.'

Serrald leaned over the table, his face between his hands.

'So it's true,' he said drearily, as if to himself, it isn't that I'm going mad. All this hasn't been subjective. Sit down, Masters. I know whom you've seen. You're right, too. He was a Territorial officer, and he's just come from his drill-hall. But his drill-hall's in hell.'

Masters stared at him and privately reflected that he was going mad.

'You're full of happy thoughts to-night,' he remarked pleasantly. 'Made a start on that book? No, of course you haven't! But I see you're still experimenting with that cipher I invented.'

'You didn't invent it!' Serrald snarled.

'My dear fellow! Don't rob me of my only claim to literary fame.'

'You didn't invent it. It was put into your head so that you could come and torture me with it. I've always avoided spiritualists and clairvoyants, and people who think they get messages from the dead by automatic writing and ouijah boards, and—and so forth. And that night, when I pulled out cards at random and applied your beastly code'

Masters interrupted him with a half-angry laugh.

'Oh, don't be a fool! You happened when I was there that night to make two inconsequent words'

'I didn't!' Serrald interrupted fiercely, 'I made one, and that wasn't inconsequent to me. Monkland is a man's name, you know.'

Masters stood and stated at him.

'I don't see why I shouldn't tell you,' Serrald continued drearily, 'I don't feel any shame now. I'm in a state of terror, and terror, if you get it badly enough, carries you miles beyond shame. Some fellows got like that in the War. I didn't, though I was bad enough, Heaven knows!

'I think you know most of my War history. I didn't join until pretty late—my department kept me—and when I did, I went to one of those Territorial regiments which had a reputation for being "particular", and for filling up with professional men and old public schoolboys. And in due time I got drafted out to France, and found myself under Monkland.

'Monkland had been out almost from the beginning. He'd been wounded twice, and after he'd risen to the rank of sergeant he'd been gazetted. Nobody denied that he was a good soldier, but everybody hated him. He was a swine to the men, and that worst kind of military brute—a martinet with a sneer. But he differed from most sneerers and loud-mouthed parade-ground flunkies. They were nearly always cowards, but he wasn't. He didn't know what fear was, and he hadn't the slightest sympathy with those who did.

'He took a special delight in bullying me and holding me up to ridicule.

I'd joined late and come out of a Government office, and I suppose I couldn't help showing how I loathed the filth and the hardship and the danger. He was the bane of my life in the rest-camps, and in the trenches. If ever there were a dirty or a dangerous job going, he put me on to it if he could. One's life, Heaven knows, was foul enough out there, without having a personal tormentor. I was in for a commission—which meant coming home for further training—but I knew he'd put a stop to that if he had the chance. And I wasn't the only one who prayed that he'd be killed.

'For all that he seemed to have a charmed life. He wasn't one of those officers who were always away on courses whenever there was any dirty work expected—because they weren't fit to lead their men. He was always on the spot, thoroughly fearless and efficient, and he seemed to love night raids. When he took one out he nearly always detailed me, because he knew how I hated them. I dare say he's listening to all this, but I don't care—I'm only telling you the truth. There's only the stark truth left between him and me now.'

He paused for breath. Masters drew his own breath slowly.

'Mad,' he thought, 'quite mad.'

'One night when we were in the Arras sector,' Serrald resumed, 'Brigade ordered a reconnaissance raid. Wanted to know if the German front line was occupied at night, and if it were they wanted a couple of prisoners—alive, if possible—as samples. Of course, Monkland got the job, and, of course, he chose me for first bayonet man. That was the kind of work I loathed—sneaking over in the dark into Heaven only knew what death-trap to try to kidnap a couple of armed men. Monkland knew how I loathed it, and it gave him a special pleasure to take me with him.

'Well, not only was the German front line occupied, but we found a machine-gun post as well. It opened out on us suddenly, and we all dodged and scattered all over the place in search of cover. The Germans must have thought that there was more considerable mischief afoot than there really was, for up went an S O S and down came a barrage.

'I lay in a shell-hole until long after everything was quiet again, not daring to come out, and at last, when I ventured, I couldn't see any of our people. Then I guessed correctly that those who were left had managed to get back to our line, and I started to try to find my way.

'It was very easy to make mistakes in the dark in No Man's Land. I must have wandered a good deal out of my way when I stumbled on a shell-hole, and there was Monkland lying in it smoking a cigarette. He was pretty badly hurt and couldn't move. He told me that he'd tried single-handed to approach the machine-gun post from the flank and bomb it, but that he'd been seen and sniped. He told me to take careful bearings of where he was and send out a stretcher party when I got back. So I left him.

'I don't know what you think of me, Masters, and I've gone a good way beyond caring. I told myself that it wasn't fair that two stretcher-bearers should risk their lives for a brute like that. All that the man had done to me clamoured in my blood for vengeance. You can guess what I did, I suppose—or what I didn't do? When I got back into our trench I didn't say anything.

'I knew it was very unlikely that Monkland would be found where he was lying. None of the raiding party seemed to know what had become of him, and the general impression was that he'd been killed or captured. A search party went out, but it only covered the ground we were supposed to have covered. So nobody ever saw Monkland alive again.

'But afterwards, long afterwards when the War was over, I knew that the cruel soul of that man still existed, that it hated me with the hatred of a devil, that it was trying desperately to make me aware of its close presence to me and its bitter enmity. For that reason I always avoided clairvoyants and people who claim to receive messages from the dead. I knew that I should get a message from Monkland. I'd been trying for years not to receive it.

'Then you brought me your cipher with the playing-cards and I pulled out some at random, and, according to your code, they spelt "Monkland". I knew that it was hopeless then. He'd got through to me. And I got bitten by an accursed morbid craving to find out what he wanted to say to me. I've hardly been able to leave the cards alone since. I've sat here by the hour, shuffling them up and picking them out at random and decoding his malignant messages to me'

'Oh, nonsense!' Masters cried, no longer able to restrain himself. 'This is sheer madness. It's unthinkable! Your mind's unhinged, Serrald.'

Serrald uttered one short, bitter laugh.

'You think so, do you? You see that heap of cards? None of them are marked, are they? Shuffle them as you like. I won't look. I'll close my eyes and turn my back. I've never been able to do a card-trick in my life. Then I'll pick out cards one by one at random and you shall see what I get.'

Masters had heard that the best way to cure a madman of his delusions was simply to disprove them to his face.

'Very well,' he said; and when Serrald had turned his back he stirred up the great heap of cards. 'What sort of messages do you generally get?' he asked unsteadily.

'The sort you might expect. Threatening, and bitter with irony and hatred. He isn't happy where he is. He wants me with him so that he can bully and pester me as he used. Are you ready? I'll close my eyes as I pick out the cards, and you shall name the code letters as I turn them.'

Masters took out a notebook and a pencil, and wrote down the letter for each card as it was turned up. He was quickly aware that actual words were being spelled, and a cold wave of horror engulfed him as soon as he began to space them. The complete message read as follows:

'Since you did not send for me, I will come for you.'

Masters uttered a sharp cry and recoiled from the table as if the cards were living and evil things.

On his way downstairs Masters met the proprietor of the house, who knew him by sight and greeted him civilly.

'Good evening, sir. Mr Serrald is pretty well, I hope?'

'No—yes,' said Masters hurriedly.

'I didn't think he had been very well lately. He has been keeping indoors a great deal and playing Patience. Is the officer gentleman with him?'

'What officer gentleman?' Masters asked through his teeth.

'The one I am always meeting on the stairs. I made sure it was Mr Serrald he's been coming to see.'

Masters said nothing, but staggered past him and out into the night.

Serrald was found dead of heart failure a few mornings later, sitting at the table before a great heap of playing-cards. It seemed that he had suspected that he might die suddenly, for he had left instructions that in such an event none of his belongings was to be touched until Masters had been sent for. The proprietor of the house met Masters in the hall, and addressed him in a hushed voice appropriate to a house of death.

'Very sudden and very sad, sir. Yes, very, very sad. He must have died sometime last night, for he was quite cold when I found him this morning. You may go up to his sitting-room, if you please, sir. He's been taken away now, but nothing else has been touched except—well, I did have the floor swept a bit. You see, sir, somebody must have come to see him last night in very muddy boots. My son, who's been a soldier and done his bit during the War, he said it was just like trench mud all over the room. You know the way up, sir?'

Masters went upstairs carrying a heart which beat harder than he had ever before known it to beat.

The chair in which Serrald had died lay on its back close to the table, on which was spread a great heap of cards lying face downwards. But along the edge of the table a few were turned face upwards in a row. Masters bent over them and shudderingly spelled out the last message which Serrald had received:

'To-night at midnight—Monkland.'

The Garden in Glenister Square

John Julian Telscombe was born in one of the houses in Glenister Square fifty-seven or fifty-eight years since. He was not quite certain of his exact age, because he was not very curious about it, and to make sure he would have had to subtract one year from another and that would have been a great deal of trouble to a man who was prematurely old and tired, and cared not in the least how old he was. You would have taken John Julian for at least seventy and, having been told of your mistake, you would have rightly surmised that his fifty-seven or fifty-eight years of life had brought with them something more than an average share of human trouble.

He had indeed fallen from comparative wealth to shabby gentility, for he had invested most of his surplus money in dubious stocks, and seen it washed away like sand in the tides of business. After the first stroke he became a little childish, and was no longer able to follow his profession. But this was neither the beginning nor the end of his troubles. Those who had known him in his better days now excused themselves for not helping him because the poor old fellow had still just enough to live on and, after all, there were many who had not. But people said that he was still fond of that worthless woman who ran away from him so long ago that even scandal had almost forgotten her.

People said that he had never been the same man again, since a certain evening, long ago, when he came home to find no wife awaiting him, and read in a curt note the story of his betrayal and knew the loneliness of all his subsequent days and nights. With that gentleness which passes for weakness in a hard world, he tried to excuse her by blaming himself. He had not always been kind to her, he said; he had been neglectful; business worries had made him irritable. Really, he avowed, the blame was his. And the world we all live in has little patience with the wronged husband who blames himself.

It was little more than a coincidence that John Julian, who had been born in Number Twelve, Glenister Square, should return to the square in the twilight of his days. His scanty resources made it necessary for him to inhabit the cheapest of furnished flats, and the top-floor of Number Sixty-three was advertised as being available at a modest rental, payable in advance. Number Sixty-three faced Number Twelve across the enclosed gardens in the middle of the square, although you could not now see one house from the other because the chestnut tree in the middle had flourished and grown ungainly since the days when John Julian was a child.

And, mark you, it was somehow appropriate that John Julian should have returned to Glenister Square, for John Julian and the square had kept pace with each other pretty evenly along the downward gradient. When John Julian was a child, Glenister Square was Glenister Square. A house in the square conferred a social position of sorts. A judge lived at Forty-eight. The houses of two baronets were only separated by the residence of Professor Mollidge, the scientist, and by their party walls. The brass plate of a very eminent doctor shone on the area railings outside Number Twenty-five. To live in Glenister Square was to obtain almost unlimited credit at the West End shops, until the West End shops learned a sharp lesson or two. Yes, these grey, Georgian houses, with their brightly painted front doors, gleaming knockers, and bell handles, and—in the summer—striped awning and geraniums in the window-boxes, had once exhaled an air of affluence, even of fashion. Nowadays—ah, well, that is a sad story.

Nowadays, the same houses look out upon the same gardens sheepishly and shabby, like shady and half-ashamed characters who have seen better days. Nobody occupies a whole house in Glenister Square today. One by one they have been converted into blocks of offices, flats, and single rooms. In the house where the judge lived a furtive doctor now conducts his practice; above him, a lawyer does anything the law allows, and sometimes just a little more. The book-maker with six telephones on the top floor, who at least pays his losses, may still claim to be the only honest man in the house.

The police know all about the roulette table on the second floor of the house in which John Julian was born. Someday soon the house will be raided; at least, that is the opinion of the shabby actor and his flamboyant lady who live on the floor below. The houses are alike—dismal on the outside and disreputable within. That is Glenister Square today.

But the railed-in gardens in the middle, where once John Julian played in holland overalls with such children of the square whose mammas could claim the same social standing as his own mamma, these gardens have altered little. A fund is still forthcoming from some mysterious source which pays the wages of a bent old man with a Sussex accent who works therein. Thus daffodils still lend a warm yellow gleam to the drab colourings of early March, and the book-maker in regarding them is reminded of the Lincolnshire Handicap and knows that Spring is not far off.

Once upon a time every householder in the square had a key to the gardens, and on fine afternoons they were the haunts of nursemaids and pretty children. And sometimes even the fathers and mothers and grown-up brothers and sisters of the children came there to take the air, sitting on rustic benches and hidden from vulgar eyes by the long shrubberies planted inside the railings. John Julian remembered how Sir Charles's daughter used to walk the paths with that Captain Leverick before, as his nurse said, 'they went and got married'. John Julian was very young then. Not until he was very much older did he understand why these two walked so slowly and why they whispered. Nowadays, nobody seems to use the gardens except the old gardener. The tenants of the houses still own keys, or have mislaid them, but the sub-tenants rest content with an outside view of the green square. For Glenister Square is given over to those who have little use for gardens; and so it was when John Julian returned.

The old man's memory—for under the circumstances I must beg leave to call John Julian an old man—was fickle. It brightened and dulled like an April landscape, so that sometimes the square seemed strange to this revenant, and sometimes it was so familiar as to cause a tightening of the throat which brought sudden moisture to the eyes. Often in wandering around the square he found himself, as if in obedience to an old unbroken habit, about to mount the steps of Number Twelve. Behind the dirty window of the room which he still called the dining-room he sometimes caught the gleam of his father's cigar. And once he looked up sharply and eagerly, with a smile on his face and a look as if his youth had momentarily been renewed, because he heard so clearly his mother's voice calling to him from an upper window.

From outside the railings he could see into his old playground. He knew the wanderings of all those hidden paths which dived into shrubberies and reappeared flanked by lawns and flower-beds. The laburnum tree in the north corner still flourished. It had deputised for stumps and bails in games of cricket played with a soft ball and a miniature bat. It had been called 'home' for the purposes of a game called hide-and-seek but, mind you, you had to be touching it fairly before your pursuer grabbed you. And sometimes egg-hat was played at its base, and this game which scored no points and owned no champion was perhaps the best of all. The thrower tossed the ball into one of a row of hats and ran for his life. The owner of the selected hat had then to pick out the ball and attempt to strike the thrower. In this game the little girls were at a disadvantage, for they threw less accurately than the boys, and their wide straw hats provided easier targets.

Sometimes John Julian remembered the name of one of those children who had been his earliest friends. He had good reason for remembering Gwennie—Gwennie who had always been so fickle, so wilful and so wayward. He remembered Gwennie as a child, always a little scornful of him, accepting his adoration as a right, and always with an air of being ready to transfer her allegiance to any newcomer who was more amusing. He remembered Gwennie at sixteen, already half a woman and coquetting with the clumsy, coltish, Charterhouse boy who was John Julian in those distant days. But best of all he remembered Gwennie in the flower of her beauty, with a strange melting sweetness in her eyes, and the softest arms which ever yet imprisoned a man's neck. Whatever had happened after that she had loved him once if only for a very little while. The Fates, in spiting him, could not take that away. They might even destroy the memory, but never the fact. John Julian had loved and been loved and he had had his hour.

As for the other children, sometimes their faces were dim and vague as reflections seen in water, and their names eluded John Julian. But sometimes he saw them as clearly with the eye of his memory as if only one yesterday separated him from them, and their names came back, bringing with them the scene and savour of those good days when life seemed one long hour of play.

There was Bobby Forsyth, with a scar over his eye, at the origin of which he hinted darkly and untruthfully when they played at Indians. Then there was Dicky Ryder, who had such a gift for spinning yarns, and ought properly to have become a popular novelist. Poor Dicky! Drowned in the Thames in trying to rescue a woman who had thrown herself from the Embankment.

And there was Willy Harkett, who afterwards got rid of his lisp, and fell riddled with bullets at the head of his own battalion. Reggie and Paul Harrison, Owen Sharp, Frank Hopgood, and half a dozen more—what had become of them? John Julian wondered whether any of them ever returned to look at the old square, and whether he would know them again.

His memory, such as it was, was less constant to the girls. Gwennie's face shone out through the years like the moon among pale clouds. Sometimes he dimly remembered Elsie Gamer, who had always been so nice to him, and whom he knew at the back of his small mind to be a better girl than Gwennie. Only he never loved Elsie and he had always loved Gwennie, and there was no more to be said. There was Marjorie Forsyth, too, and Winnie Ryder, and still others—mere girls who were permitted, often not too courteously, to take part in the pastimes of the sterner sex. Often as he wandered around the square, the ghost of John Julian's lost youth stirred within him as if it wanted to escape and go into the locked-up gardens to find shadowy playmates.

Not until some weeks after his return to the square did John Julian remember It. Some trick of his defective memory had withheld from him the awesome recollection. And even in the old days when he was a child, if you had asked him what It was he would not have been able to tell you. All the children who played in those gardens had their own ideas on the subject, all vague and shapeless and awesome, and all utterly different.

It was Dicky Ryder, the spinner of yarns, who had invented It. It lived in the deep parts of the shrubbery where it was dark even in the daytime. It was never seen, but unless you were very careful you were always liable to see It, and then woe betide you! It had no name; it was simply called 'It'; and that added to Its terrors. When laurel leaves stirred mysteriously, It was aware of your presence, and then it was time to run.

For Dicky had the artistry of the born teller of tales. Had he merely described some bogey or monster and given it a name, he would have produced very little effect on his audience. But in avowing himself as being quite unable to describe It, and giving It no name but It, he allowed many youthful imaginations to run riot and thus multiplied Its creepy horrors a thousandfold.

To be sure he had plenty of tales to tell about It, none of which was particularly bright or pleasant. They mostly concerned boys and girls who lived in the square years before, and had gone into the shrubbery never to return. They had simply disappeared. It had got them.

John Julian remembered, with a smile, how, after the invention of It, the children had taken to forming couples when games of hide-and-seek sent them into the shrubberies. And sometimes the little girls asked to hold the hands of the little boys for greater safety, a comfort they were often graciously permitted on the understanding that nothing was said about it afterwards.

It was tantalising to John Julian to be debarred from re-entering his old playground. The gates were always locked even when the old gardener was at work inside. Once or twice he hailed the gardener, but, discovering him to be almost stone deaf, he did not persevere. The shrubberies had spread a great deal, and its strongholds were enlarged. He tried to recollect what he had once fancied It to be like. He wondered how Dicky Ryder, who plainly believed in his own invention, had pictured It. Now he could half believe that the boy had inherited a strain of memory from some far-distant ancestor and had re-created Pan, the god of the undergrowths, of Nature, and of stark fear. For nearly four months John Julian lived in the top flat of Number Sixty-three, and dreamed fitfully in his sleep of Gwennie as a child, and of other children more dimly portrayed, and sometimes of the dreadful, shadowy, shapeless shape of It.

It was late in the summer. All the day rain had fallen intermittently on London, and thunder had rolled over it. The heat had been stifling—that muggy, oppressive heat which cannot be gauged by the thermometer. But after sunset the skies and the air cleared. Stars began to blink and sparkle over the city, and cool breezes, like compassionate angels, flew in at windows and passed through stuffy streets, caressing hot foreheads and breathing whispers of far-off woods and flowers and running streams. John Julian had sat and stifled in his attic sitting-room all day, watching the play of lightning across his little window, and seeing the still tree-tops in the gardens limned against a leaden sky. But when darkness had fallen, and the storm had spent itself in grumbling, and the Great Bear looked into his window from the north, he took his hat and stick and tottered downstairs with an old man's gait, and went shambling through the delicious coolness that awaited him out of doors.

He had then been back in Glenister Square for close upon four months, and his habit was to walk around the square at least once before going to bed, sometimes whistling back memories which were better left astray. Tonight it was a sheer joy to be out in the air, for the gardens expressed their thanks for the rain and coolness in the most delicious way. John Julian could smell wet earth and grass and flowers and evergreens all blended together. And although it was such a night of stars and sweet scents John Julian was the only living thing afoot on the south side of the square.

But when he reached the first comer and turned he saw in the lamplight the figure of a woman, and she drew him up at once from a great bank of shadows close to the railings. She was elderly and bedraggled, and carried a tray of matches in her hand. There was despair in every line of her, and in her walk, and, when she spoke, he was to hear it in her voice. For she was too listless to assume the whine of the professional beggar, and her voice was natural and dreadful to hear.

'For God's sake buy a box of matches, sir! I'm wet and starving, and no money to buy food, and no bed to go to.'

John Julian halted and looked into her face. It was not a good face. She was one of the off-scourings of a great city, pretty once, no doubt, and delicate and tender to touch, and had loved gaiety and beauty to her own undoing. But most of the evil he saw on the face upturned to his had been written there by want.

He felt in his pockets for loose coppers, and as he did so he thought:

'What use if I give this woman a few coppers? She will have her cup of tea and her slab of bread, but she will still be homeless and wet and almost as hungry.'

He felt in another pocket in which he knew there was a pound note. He really did not know how to spare it until the next instalment of his annuity came in. But for Gwennie's sake he paused no more than a second. For Gwennie's sake he was kind and gentle to all women, because she still represented womanhood in his eyes, and because he had a strange illogical belief that a kindness done to any woman was a kindness to her. He did not know if she were living or dead, but to John Julian every member of her sex represented this lost love of his.

The woman's hand closed over the note, and at the same moment a strange whinnying cry of surprise and delight broke from her lips and was infinitely pitiful to hear.

'God bless you!' she said fervently. 'God bless you!'

Now as she said these words the strangest of sensations came to John Julian. He felt himself falling, and then looked around him in surprise to find that he had not fallen. And the woman was holding up her tray, and the light of youth was in her eyes, and the evil which he had seen in her face was all gone.

'Take one,' she whispered. 'You must take one.'

John Julian stared at the tray.

'Why!' he exclaimed, i thought you were selling matches.'

For on the tray was a pile of keys, which were all old keys and looked alike, as if they were made to fit the same lock.

'Take one,' said the woman, 'and you will find it the key to your heart's desire.'

He took one, wondering, and as he did so he recognised it, and partly understood. For this key was made to open any of the locked gates of the gardens, so that he was dimly aware that something very improbable had happened, and that by this key he might win back to his lost childhood. But his gaze was attracted from the key to the woman's face, for in her he now saw suddenly a faint, elusive, wavering likeness of Gwennie.

He spoke the name twice in a voice which changed its key because of his wonder and delight, and drew towards her; but as he stepped forward it seemed that she drew back from him; and by the railings, in the massed shadows of the laurels, he found himself alone.

He stood calling her a little while, but had no answer, and the two roads branching from the comer were alike empty. Then, thinking that perhaps she had already gone before him into the garden, he went to the nearest gate, fitted the key, and opened it. Then, carefully, as he had been taught as a child, he locked the gate behind him.

It was while he was locking the gate that another change came over John Julian, and not only over him but over his surroundings. For the sun of an afternoon in May blazed suddenly over the gardens and over a little boy in a holland smock who stood locking the gate behind him. For John Julian had travelled far back along the years in a space of time too brief for measurement, and he was not in the least surprised at finding himself a little boy again, because with the change he had forgotten that he had ever been anything else.

And when he had locked the gate he ran whooping to the diagonally opposite comer of the gardens, because he was a little late, and he was afraid lest the others might have started some game without him. But he found them gathered round a faded green seat, and they were not playing, but talking very gravely together, so that he guessed at once that Dick Ryder had been telling them a story.

Bobby Forsyth sat in the middle of the seat between Owen and Frank, with Elsie perched on one of its curved arms. They were all there: Marjorie and her two smaller sisters, Paul, Willy, and Dick Ryder—all except Gwennie, and one glance proclaimed to him her absence.

'Oh, here he is!' said one of them, and then there was a sudden silence as if they had been talking of John Julian.

'Where's Gwennie?' he asked.

'You'd better ask that boy who's just come to live at Number Five,' said Marjorie cruelly; and John Julian wriggled uncomfortably and looked away, because he was jealous and did not want the others to see.

'We'd better tell him,' said Bobby, the acclaimed leader, scowling around him. 'Come here, young John Julian.'

Now, John Julian was aware that something very unpleasant was toward, so he coloured, and said:

'Shan't! Come here yourself!'

'If I have to come and fetch you, you'll be sorry!' said Bobby, his scowl deepening.

And then Dicky Ryder, who stood by the seat bouncing a tennis-ball, looked up at John Julian, and called out to him.

'I'm sticking up for you,' he said. 'Better come and hear the rot they want to talk. Bobby's an awful ass! In fact, they all are.'

Dicky could afford to speak of Bobby in those terms, he being the only one with any chance against him in a fight. John Julian was grateful to him for his championship, and came forward into the circle of children.

'If you've come to look for Gwennie,' began Bobby, 'you can go elsewhere. We've sent her to Coventry. She isn't coming into the gardens any more. She's lost her key, and one of us always had to let her in, so now we can keep her out. And if she does manage to get in, we shall all go. See? And if you have anything to do with her, we'll send you to Coventry, too!'

John Julian's face grew longer and longer as he listened, and he felt the tears rising very close under his eyes.

'Oh, why?' he burst out.

Then one of the little girls uttered a laugh which sounded very hard, coming from a child, and said, 'Well, you ought to know!'

'It's John Julian's business,' said Dicky Ryder wearily, 'and I think you're a set of asses. Why can't you let them alone?'

'We're not going to let kids behave just as they like,' declared Bobby.

'And if John Julian's mug enough to stand it, we're not going to stand him'.'

'But what's she done?' John Julian cried in an agony.

'She's always been your special friend,' said Bobby. 'You've always shared things with her and done everything for her. And now there's a new boy come to live here she's always about with him and won't look at you. She doesn't know the first thing about playing cricket, and we're not going to stand it. She can go and play by herself, and if you don't like it you can go and play by yourself, too.'

John Julian looked around him and saw assent on every face except Dicky's. And the faces of the little girls were hardest of all, which seemed strange to him, he being only a child.

'But it's my business!' John Julian wailed, i couldn't be happy unless she was happy. And if I forgive'

'Forgive!' echoed Bobby with deep contempt; and there was a chorus of laughter.

'So,' Owen chimed in, 'you can just please yourself. You always were a bit soft.'

John Julian choked once or twice, and a bitter sense of injustice rose within him.

'I hate you all!' he cried out. 'All except Dicky. I shall always be Gwennie's friend. She—she'll—she'll be friends with me again someday. And I'm not going to let you send her to Coventry.'

At this there was another general laugh, and Bobby, grinning with the knowledge of his power, asked him:

'And how are you going to stop us, silly?'

'I'll fight you!' cried John Julian, and raised another laugh; for it was well-known that John Julian was no fighter at all.

'And I'll fight him afterwards,' remarked Dicky Ryder quietly, still meditatively bouncing his tennis-ball.

'Yes, you'll do some fighting!' sneered Bobby Forsyth. 'You'll'

He broke off abruptly and sprang up, for at that moment John Julian rushed blindly at him and clung to him about the middle, with no idea of what he should do next. There was laughter and a scream or two, words of encouragement, and then sudden silence.

The silence came as suddenly and sharply as the stroke of a sword, and with it there came upon John Julian a feeling of awe, almost of terror. And he was aware, too, that his antagonist felt some similar sensation, for the expected blow never fell, and slowly John Julian unwound his arms and stood upright and furtively looked about him.

The children all stood as still as so many little statues, each in an attitude of listening. The afternoon sun blazed over the gardens, which had become suddenly as still as a graveyard at dead of night. John Julian was at first aware of no sound at all, but as he strained his ears he caught a faint stirring of leaves from the laurels close at hand, and a panic which gagged his tongue and bound his limbs came upon him, for he knew what this meant. It was moving in the laurels. It was about to emerge. They were going to see it at last.

John Julian's and every other pair of eyes were staring fixedly at the laurels whence came these faint, ominous rustlings. And now the outer leaves shivered and parted, and something white became visible, gleaming behind them. Slowly and heavily, like some lethargic monster rising from his bed, one limb at a time, so did It emerge from the laurels into the sunlight.

Now this creature was made in the shape of a great man, and yet it was not entirely human. It wore only a loin-cloth of skin and its naked limbs and body gleamed with the whiteness of polished marble, and but for this strange shining It might have been a stone god out of an old garden come suddenly to life. Its face was a man's face, and yet not a man's, for It was wholly devoid of expression, like an unfinished piece of sculpture, and It moved slowly and laboriously as if Its limbs and joints were of stone. It stood towering above the children, looking down on them, intelligently and yet still without expression, with neither kindness nor malice on Its face. Then It spoke, and Its voice was as expressionless as Its face and deep and sharp like the falling of great stones heard far down in a deep cavern.

'Some difficulty vexes you,' It said, 'I will decide.'

'Yes. It must decide.'

It was Dicky Ryder's voice which piped up, and It looked at him.

'Ah,' he said, 'here is the one who is not afraid of me.'

'I am not afraid of you,' said Dicky, 'because I made you.'

'Yes, you made me. Everybody made me. But only a few can understand. You are a teller of tales. You understand much, and few will ever understand you, and so you will never be very happy.'

And Dicky looked up into the stone face and laughed as if he had known this all the while and it did not trouble him.

'You know why these two were fighting,' Dicky said,

'Indeed I do. For I heard everything. And you, you teller of tales, and John Julian here are both wrong; for all these others are right. And the girl you have spoken of must never again be allowed into the garden nor into any of your games. For this little boy here is a fool, and fools must be protected even against themselves. And if you, John Julian, think otherwise, then you must share her exile, and perhaps take your share alone.'

At this many of the children took heart, and smiled up into the face of stone.

And it was mostly the little girls who smiled. John Julian looked up, too, and his eyes were steadfast while his mouth drooped.

'But if I cannot be happy without her?' he urged.

'Then you must leave the garden.'

'Is that fair?'

'Poor fool!'

Then John Julian spoke again, and what he said he scarcely knew, but he was strangely aware that he was talking like a man and that a man's voice controlled his tongue.

'Yes, I am a fool,' he said slowly; 'but at least I know you. I know what you are!'

'And what am I?' It asked.

Then John Julian went on talking like a man.

'i know without being able to say, and that is not strange for no one could exactly say. You are neither god nor devil; you are infinitely less than either. You are not even Nature. There is nothing infinite in you. But you are a part of Nature. You are something that is in all of us, and you are sometimes good and sometimes bad, and utterly incomprehensible. You are the instinct in man which makes one who has been nobly moved by music go home and thrash a dog. You are the instinct which makes a man who has lately come from committing a brutal crime sit in a theatre and applaud Virtue and hiss Vice as he sees it depicted on the stage. There is neither logic nor justice in you, and yet you are still human. You are so human that you wear that face of stone—because you can be moved so easily to laughter and to tears.'

And it looked down upon John Julian, still without expression, and said nothing.

Then in the silence there arose a voice crying outside the nearest gate, and it cried piteously, saying:

'Let me in! Let me in!'

And John Julian recognised the voice of Gwennie, and he saw the child outside with her loose hair tumbled over one shoulder, wrenching at the bars of the gate. And he cried out to her joyfully and waved his hand, and had taken a step towards her when the voice of It arrested him.

'Where are you going?' It asked.

John Julian looked up into Its face.

'You know!' he said.

And Dicky Ryder murmured like an echo:

'Yes. It knows.'

'You are going out to her because she may not come in?'

'Yes.'

'You will be very wretched.'

'Am I not bound to be wretched, whatever I do?'

'Poor fool!'

'No. I would be nothing else than a fool, since it seems that only fools may forgive the trespasses against themselves.'

So saying, John Julian walked to the gate, and his step was as light as the step of a man who goes to a great happiness; and his heart was full of a great love for the pathetic little creature clamouring at the bars.

'I'm so sorry! Forgive! I'm so sorry!' she sobbed; the same words over and again. And John Julian, fumbling with the key and almost bereft of words, could only stammer:

'My dear! My dear!'

He had pulled open the gate when a voice behind him cried:

'Stay!'

And against his will, he looked round and up into the face of It.

'I must decide,' said It. i do not know whether it is just for you to go out to her in exile, or whether it is just to allow her back into the garden. For, as you have said, I know nothing of justice, and you, being a fool, care nothing where it concerns yourself. But I know something of happiness and a great deal of fools, and therefore, since your happiness depends on her, you must bring her into the garden. For as you have also said, I am still human, and can be moved so easily to laughter and to tears.'

And as It spoke Its face relaxed and became no longer a face of stone. And It wore a look of great gentleness and sweetness, and the mouth became beautiful in smiling, and in the eyes there was pity and perfect understanding; and Its face shone.

John Julian gazed for a moment on this sudden and gracious change, and then he turned to Gwennie and gathered her into his arms. He felt her tears on his cheek and heard her crying for forgiveness, and would have answered her, but there was no need for him to speak. Just then he was aware of another change. He and Gwennie were no longer children. They were man and woman who stood clasped together on the threshold of the open gate in an ecstasy which was sharper than pain. A great distance away he heard the voice of the beggar-woman saying:

'God bless you.'

Then gently he drew Gwennie over the stone threshold of the gardens.

A policeman found John Julian lying dead outside the railings of the gardens in Glenister Square. He was brought to the spot by a beggar-woman who said that the poor gentleman had dropped down while in the act of taking a box of matches which he had just bought from her.

The Affair at Paddock Cross

'I knew beyond all doubt that I had been warned, that I had dreamed the reality of a hundred-and-fifty years ago, and that, unless I heeded, tragedy was to follow.'

'Before opening my eyes I was aware that my hand was in the clasp of another, and when I opened them I saw that my wrist was being held over a basin into which my blood was trickling. I was lying on a couch opposite high windows, through which I could see flowering lilacs waving in sun and wind. Not for a full minute did I remember the collision at Paddock Cross when my chaise and the other, both wildly driven, had met wheel to wheel.

So much came back to me while my gaze travelled to the worsted- covered legs and dull shoe-buckles of the little surgeon. I still had no thought of where I was. It was a fair room, furnished after the French style of the day. There was a gilt arm to the couch on which I rested and gilt legs to the chairs. Where ever I might be I was in an environment of wealth and refinement. The little surgeon perceived that my eyes were open and exclaimed aloud in satisfaction.

'Aha!' said he. 'There is naught to better a little blood-letting for a fit of swooning. Have no fear, sir; you are in skilled hands, though I dare say it.'

And he chuckled like one who was proud of his trade.

I regarded him, though with but little interest, from his unpowdered wig to his worn shoes. His coat was off, and the sleeves of his shirt were rolled above his elbows. I noticed that one of his breeches was unbuttoned at the knee.

'Where am I?' I asked.

'The guest of my Lord Stevenbury,' he answered. 'He had you conveyed hither and summoned me instanter. My lord was in the other chaise. He had been over to Powers Court and lost a wager and a grand game bird. A spring of his carriage breaks on the way back, so he must needs leave it at the Crown and have out a chaise. I make no doubt that he ordered the boy to travel like a Bedlamite; and yours, if I hear truly, was no loiterer.'

While he talked the little man sealed my wrist and applied a bandage.

'What of my boy?' I asked.

'Alas! Poor Tom Hammett has posted his last stage. They will miss him on these roads. A pretty whip, sir, a pretty whip, but not the first pretty whip to come to grief at Paddock Cross.'

I moved my head and was requited by a sharp stab of pain. I winced, and realised that my skull was heavily bandaged.

'You are fortunate, sir,' said the little man, laying aside the basin. 'Your stars have been kind to you. The chaise is a wreck, the boy and the leader dead, and here you be with no worse than a cracked head. But I hear my lord outside. This will be good news for him.'

He skipped to the door to open it, but was forestalled. It was not my lord who entered first, but a lady, whom I guessed rightly to be his wife. She was a tall, dark woman of proud bearing, her lips a little too full and ripe in strong contrast to the pallor of her cheeks. Her eyes under dark arched brows were black or the very deepest brown, and they were full of such an exquisite pity and compassion that my heart clamoured as if to reach hers.

There followed her into the room a big, dark-browed man in a green travelling coat and breeches. He was broad of shoulder, long of limb, and upright as a soldier; but he had an ill face to contrast with his fine figure. It was a face blotched and swollen with those dissipations to which idle gentlemen are prone. Yet he regarded me kindly enough and stepped towards me with an air of courtesy and pity.

'You are recovered a little?' he asked. 'Sir, I thank Heaven for that. Heaven knows to whom you apportion the blame, but I know where to lay it. Paddock Cross is a peril to the King's passengers. I have said it a thousand times. I will have the road straightened. I will have it straightened if it costs a thousand guineas. I will not be baulked by any parish council. They shall know who is their master!'

And with that he broke into a volley of oaths which were unfit for the ears of his lady, although she seemed to hear them unmoved. I was not squeamish, but they stabbed my sore head like blows of a knife. All the while I was aware of her eyes seeking mine.

'My lord,' I said, 'for I take it that I have the honour of addressing my Lord Stevenbury'—at which he bowed—'I am vastly obliged for your hospitality and for the surgical aid which you were so kind as to procure for me. I am now a little recovered and, with your leave, able to make a short journey'

He cut me short with a protesting hand.

'No, sir. I'll not hear of it. You must stay our guest until your recovery is complete.' He turned to the surgeon. 'Taylor, tell him he must not go. It would imperil his life. Tell him, Taylor.'

'Nay, my lord,' answered the surgeon. 'I'll not be answerable. A jolt or two along the roads and I'll not be answerable.'

He turned to me triumphantly.

'You heard him, sir. He'll not be answerable. You are very welcome, sir. You shall not be plagued with formalities. Rise, sleep and eat when you will, win back to perfect health at Nature's leisure.'

'Yes,' said the lady, just loud enough for me to hear, 'he must stay.'

It was because of her I stayed. I own to it. Him I hated from the first, knowing—as I knew full well—that those gestures of hospitality came of an over-weening vanity. He could do no less than bid me stop. He would not have men say that my Lord Stevenbury had turned a man from his door in such bodily straits as mine. I thanked him in such terms as came readily to my tongue.

'Lord knows,' he said, i would not plague you with idle questions, but if you will be so good as to tell me whom I have the honour to entertain'

So I told him that I was Captain Hebden, of the Royal Hussars, and on my way to visit my mother in Dorsetshire when the accident befell. At which he bowed gravely and said:

'Captain Hebden, I am most happy to meet you. I wish only that I were indebted to some more fortunate chance for the pleasure of your acquaintanceship.'

After which he presented me to his lady; who would suffer me to make no attempt to rise. Her tone was courteous with even a note of coldness, but my lord, who stood by, could not see the eyes which she turned upon me. No man had called me Lothario, but then none had called me Joseph.

Later two of my lord's footmen carried me to bed and I laid my aching head to rest in a chamber on the south side, with lavender-scented curtains to shield me from the early-morning sunlight.

Here memory leaves me for a time. No, not leaves me, but stands apart. There are mists which obscure the eye of memory as there are sometimes mists in the air which thwart the natural vision.

I think I recovered slowly. Days passed, many days, and I was still my lord's guest. Day after day the house was filled with drunken gambling squires; either that or my lord was absent, drinking and gambling elsewhere. My lady sat clean and calm above these orgies, a water-lily in a mud-pool. My hurts excused me from taking part in these drunken carousals, and I became my lady's friend and constant companion. I know that she begged me to call her Clarissa, but not when my lord was by. I see all these things as through a glass darkly, and hear her voice as through the ravings of a storm. When my lord was absent we would sit in shade beside a round stone garden pond, where golden carp came close to the surface at the sun's wooing. There sometimes I would read to her from the poets or we would tell each other of our lives. I had seen enough of my lord to make it hard for me to keep my hands from his throat, and there was little of her present life with him that I needed hearing. She told me that whatever love she had once borne him had died long since.

'Love does not die,' I said. 'The flame from the burnt-out ember seeks more fuel.'

There came an afternoon when I was well-recovered and my lady and I sat by the fish pond. My lord was away at a friend's cockpit, with two game birds in bags which his servant carried. Clarissa put into my hands a book from which she bade me read to her.

'It is called "An Elegy Written in a Country Churchyard",' she said, it is a poem which catched poor Wolfe so mightily last year.'

So I read, but after a while my thoughts could not follow the words, and suddenly my voice broke like a boy's, and I was in her arms. We might have been Francesca and Paola embracing for the first time over the tale of Guinevere.

Then came the rustle of leaves and the fall of a heavy foot, and my lord stood before us, bowing with a fine irony in smile and gesture. My lady hid her white face in her white hands, rose and walked apart with him.

'Captain Hebden,' said he, with a grin of malice, 'permit me to tell you that you have some original notions in the matter of repaying hospitality.'

'Hardly original,' I answered him; 'but then you have likely not heard of the siege of Troy. I wish I could say that your lack of learning was your least admirable trait.'

'I'll have your heart on my sword, Paris,' he said, through his teeth, 'but not for insolence.'

'You will not,' I gave him back, if you challenge me, I choose pistols.'

He thought for a moment.

'There is an inn in the village good enough for the likes of you,' he said at last. 'Go there, and my friend shall wait upon you within the hour. You shall meet me, never fear. I waive the fact that you are no gentleman. One can't afford to be over-nice.'

And in an hour we met. We stood ten paces apart, watching for the fall of a white handkerchief which fluttered in the wind. Taylor, the surgeon, was there, white of face, and his mouth grimacing with apprehension.

Then the handkerchief fell and the darkness swallowed me.

When I recovered consciousness I found myself propped up on a long chesterfield, with cushions under the head which the doctor had just finished bandaging. He was a typical country doctor, old-fashioned enough to wear pince-nez and modem enough to wear a blazer.

'Hallo!' he said; 'how are we feeling?'

'We're feeling rotten, thanks,' I answered. 'Would you mind telling me what happened and where I am?'

'You had a nasty smash-up in your car,' he answered. 'But don't worry. I was afraid of concussion at first, but you're all right. And you're now at Mr Welling's place, Datcham Hall. It was his car you hit, and he brought you here—or, rather, he got the people in the next car that came along to be good Samaritans. And now you mustn't talk too much. You're quite all right.'

It all came back to me now, but I was struggling to loosen other memories. I did not immediately remember my dream—if I must call it a dream. Quite certainly I had never before visited a house called Datcham Hall, nor did I know a Mr Welling. And yet the room was vaguely familiar, although the furniture was strange. I felt that I knew its shape, the position of the three doors, but most of all the high windows facing me. Through them I could see rhododendrons in full flower, and I felt that they ought to have been lilac-trees. And then a little, a very little, of it came back to me.

The doctor was speaking. He said:

'That's a ghastly spot to people who don't know the road, and even to those who do—that narrow hairpin bend just before you come to Paddock Cross. We have accidents there every year.'

Something in my memory leaped at the mention of Paddock Cross.

'Will you tell me something, doctor?' I asked. 'I'm beginning to remember a most peculiar dream I had while I was unconscious. I'm a stranger here, and I'd never heard of Paddock

Cross until I dreamed it just now and then you mentioned it. And I seem to know this room, although I can't have been in it before. My head aches like sin and I hate being puzzled'

'Well, then,' he interrupted, 'don't puzzle, and don't ask me to account for the vagaries of your sub-conscious mind. Probably you had gleams of returning consciousness which faded out again and left you with the material for a dream. Now just you lie quiet and don't trouble about anything, until I can get you moved to the Cottage Hospital '

A woman's voice proceeding through an open door interrupted him.

'Oh, no, doctor. Will that be necessary? Can't he stay here?'

I knew that voice and with an unpleasant sensation very like dread, I knew that I should recognise its owner. Nor was I deceived. The woman who stepped softly across the room was Lady Stevenbury, wearing a tweed suit of today's fashion; but the doctor addressed her as Mrs Welling.

'I'm so glad you're feeling better already,' she said to me, 'but you mustn't dream of moving yet. We'll take the very greatest care of you, and it's so uncomfortable in that wretched hospital. The smell of the place—scrubbing and disinfectant—gives me cold shivers. Besides, my husband says that if you hadn't kept your head you might both have been killed.'

'I was on the wrong side, I'm afraid,' announced a man's voice from the door. 'The wheel-marks prove that. Really, I don't know how to apologise, and the least you can do is to allow us to take care of you until you are better. You'll send a nurse, doctor, won't you?'

I knew that man's voice, and I knew, before I turned my eyes upon him, exactly what he was going to be like. What they saw in my face they attributed to pain and sickness.

Of course, they asked me my name, and where they could communicate with my friends and relatives. In answer to the first question I almost said 'Captain Hebden' so fresh and deep was the impression on my mind. But my name happens to be Rivers, and I am a humble man of letters. I had no near relatives to worry over my fate. There was a girl in Shropshire, but I could not risk causing her anxiety by letting them write to her. Later, they helped me to bed but it was not in the same room which I had occupied 'before'.

I passed a restless night. Between fitful snatches of sleep I tried to find some sane explanation of it all. It was quite reasonable to suppose that in some fleeting return to semi-consciousness I had heard mention of Paddock Cross, seen my host and hostess, and had so contrived to weave a vivid and disagreeable dream. But in my dream I had been so much at home in the part of Captain Hebden. His character—which was never mine—I had worn like a glove. I had taken over his points of view, even his memories. And, stranger still, how had I come to dream the characters of Mr and Mrs Welling? It did not need much knowledge of psychology to assure me that they were twentieth century editions of my 'Lord and Lady Stevenbury'. I clung to all the cliches I had heard about the 'depths and workings of the sub-conscious mind', but I was not satisfied. I could not wholly believe that I had merely dreamed. For a week I lay in bed. Mrs Welling nursed me most of the time, and I don't think

Welling altogether liked it. He came up to see me sometimes and spoke to her in a way that made me wince. Generally he struck me as not being altogether sober, but he carried his liquor well enough to pass muster, and his offensiveness to his wife was subtle rather than blatant.

The Wellings, I gather, were not nouveaux riches. They both belonged to minor County families of no very great antiquity. Mrs Welling grew very confidential with me. She told me, although not in so many words, that she was not on the best of terms with 'dear Hugh'; and when a woman drops that kind of hint to another man she does not do it for the mere sake of talking.

She was a great lover of poetry, so she said, and allowed me to visualise her husband as a hard-working, hard-drinking Philistine. I can't deny her fascination. More than once it was brought home to me with a swift shock that a man might easily lose his head over her.

On the eighth day after the accident I was allowed to come downstairs to lunch. The dining-room was long, narrow and panelled in oak; and one of its two fireplaces had armorial bearings carved on it. It was Welling who pointed this out to me.

'Those,' he said, 'are the arms of the Stevenbury family, now extinct. The place used to belong to them.'

In the same instant I saw him regarding me strangely, not without cause. I must have shown him the oddest face that a man could wear.

'Sure you feel all right now you're up?' he asked solicitously. 'Hadn't you better turn in again?'

I was in two minds myself, but I sat down to luncheon with them. My head swam every time I thought of this fresh coincidence. Stevenbury! I could not have dreamed that name! Or, rather, how had I come to dream it?

Theories, which seemed too outrageous to contemplate, thrust themselves on my unwilling mind. Prudence told me that I ought to go, that I ought to make some excuse for leaving that house at all costs and immediately; curiosity urged me to stay and mark what happened next.

Towards the end of the meal Welling said to me:

'I'm awfully sorry, but I've got to go out this afternoon. However, my wife will look after you.'

'I'll try,' said Mrs Welling demurely.

And he went. I had a vision-like memory of another man—or was it, after all, the same?—setting forth on just such an afternoon with a servant and two game-cocks. Mrs Welling accompanied me into the cool, lofty hall.

'What do you want to do?' she asked simply.

'I think, if you don't mind very much, I want to rest.'

'Then why not rest out of doors? It's beautiful outside.'

I excused myself as gracefully as I could, and said that I would rather go to my room.

'Very well,' she said, a faint note of disappointment creeping into her tone. 'I am going to take a book into the fresh air. I shall be in the lower garden.'

So I mounted to my room, but I could not rest. My head turned and turned again. I wanted desperately to know more—to prove my dream, or warning, or reincarnation—call it what I choose—or to know beyond doubt that I was being hoaxed by my own subconscious self. So, after an hour's indecision, I went downstairs and out into the gardens behind the house.

I found her sitting on a long white garden seat backed by a low shrubbery, and facing a shallow round pond. I knew that stone basin which held the water, although its dry margin was cracked now and lichen eaten. I recognised it again, while all my senses cried out to reason and my heart beat like a hammer in the weak hands of a child.

Mrs Welling regarded me with lazy satisfaction and made room for me on the seat.

'I'm so glad you changed your mind,' she said. 'Do you feel better now? Come and sit down. This is my favourite spot, you know.'

She was looking at me out of her great liquid dark eyes, and I felt the lure of her. It was not the less potent for being something infinitely less than love.

I sat down beside her and shivered like a child in the rain.

There was an open book on her knees. She closed it and handed it across to me. It was the Oxford Book of English Verse.

'Won't you please read something to me?' she begged, in a low, soft, wheedling voice. 'That is to say, if it doesn't tire you. I am sure you read beautifully.'

I opened the book at random. And then I dropped it. I felt sick and faint, and I was sure my head would burst under the pressure of a rush of blood.

Very far away, it seemed, I heard Mrs Welling's voice say:

'Yes, that one, please. I never tire of it. I love Gray's "Elegy".'

I fled into the house. I said that I was ill, and I must have looked ill indeed. I knew beyond all doubt that I had been warned, that I had dreamed the reality of a hundred-and-fifty years ago, and that, unless I heeded, tragedy was to follow. History had not, and could not, repeat itself literally word for word, but history never needs to do that, having the choice of too many unpleasant variations.

That night I slipped away, leaving a note behind me. I often wonder what they thought of me, just as I often wonder precisely what would have happened had I remained, now that duelling is a dead practice.

But I did not love Mrs Welling; and besides, there was a girl down in Shropshire.

Auntie Kate

I saw at once that Master Leo Franklin did not know me from Adam. He eyed me with that sort of furtive curiosity with which shy children regard strangers. I might have been hurt had I not borne in mind that two years, which is so short a spell to a man in the fifties, is such a great length of time in the first decade of childhood.

To be truthful, I did not think he had improved. At five and a half he had been a bright, jolly, intelligent little chap. Now, at seven and a half, a queer unnatural old-mannishness had taken the place of this natural brightness, and his little face looked wan and thin and unhealthy.

We met quite by chance in the village shop, that wonderful emporium where clothes, groceries, sweets, tobacco, and stamps might be purchased. On alighting at the station I had found nobody and no vehicle to meet me. Being short of tobacco, and since I smoke a cheap kind which can be had anywhere, I had turned into the village shop to get some before walking on to the house; and there I found Master Leo pocketing a small bag of sweets while the worthy Mr Trimms counted out his change.

'Good afternoon, sir,' said Mr Trimms to me, with great cordiality.

"Tisn't often you see one of these nowadays, is it, sir?'

It was a golden sovereign which he handed across the counter for my inspection.

'It isn't, indeed,' I said. 'Where did you get it?'

He nodded down towards Leo

'Master Franklin's just changed it. He's a lucky young gentleman to have so much money.'

I examined the coin in something like amazement, for I saw something at once that had escaped the notice of the worthy Trimms. The date on the coin was 1874, and it looked like new.

Now, even in the days before this vile paper money of ours one seldom saw an old sovereign. I believe, as soon as they were worn with use and so lost weight, they were returned to the Mint. So this coin, while being worth no more than twenty shillings, was a double rarity.

'I'll give you a pound note and a shilling for it,' I said to Trimms.

'With pleasure, sir. There's some assets store by gold, I know. But it won't buy more than the paper, and a shilling's a shilling.'

So I became possessed of the coin, ordered a pound of my villainous tobacco, and then turned to Leo.

'Now, you villain,' I cried, 'how dare you forget me. Parade—t'shun!—stannat-haise!—t'shun! Why, you rascal, you've forgotten your drill already! Never mind, give me a kiss.'

I bent down and he touched my rough old cheek with his lips.

'Are you my Uncle George?' he asked.

I was no relation to the boy, but he had been brought up to call me that.

'Of course I am,' I said. 'Fancy your forgetting me!'

'It's such years since we met, isn't it?' he said, imitating his mother's delightful drawl. 'Of course you're coming to stay with us. I'm so glad. Wasn't Mummy at the station? I know she was going to drive down to meet you.'

No, there was something about the boy's self-possession which I did not like. I had promised to look after him, to be a father to him, and felt a twinge of conscience at having accepted that temporary post in the Argentine, and so neglected my job.

Time had been when I loved the boy's mother. I suppose I still did, but as one grows older these violent emotions mellow into quiet friendships. Dick Franklin, of my own regiment, had been my successful rival, but we had contrived still to be friends.

As I looked at the child the memory of a night at Gavrelle came back to me with poignant distinctness. Dick Franklin had charge of a small bombing-raid, a mere pin-prick to annoy the enemy. The enemy had retaliated by plastering our front line and supports with shells, and incidentally severing my telephone communication with the various Company headquarters. I was climbing out of Battalion Headquarters' dug-out to see what was happening, and the first I saw was two bearers labouring under a stretcher on their way to the Aid Post a few yards further down.

'It's Captain Franklin, sir,' said one of them.

He was nearly gone, but he knew me and he could just speak.

'The boy,' he said; 'you'll look after him?'

Of course I promised. Well, Dick Franklin was sleeping in the little cemetery for soldiers at Roclincourt, and here I was, and here was the boy to whom I was supposed to take a father's place. And, Heaven forgive me, I found that I didn't like him!

Oh, yes, I'd done my duty in a sort of way. I'd bought him toys; I'd helped his mother to unravel her affairs and re-invest her modest fortune, and I'd got the boy entered for her at Winchester. I liked children, but never pretended to myself that I understood them. Perhaps this one had reached some awkward phase of childhood, such as I seemed to remember hearing the parents of other children discuss.

'I expect Mummy didn't know the train was going to be so terribly punctual,' I said. 'Perhaps the best thing we can do is to go back to the station and wait for her, since she's driving down.'

He shook his head.

'Mummy doesn't like me to come into the village alone. Don't tell her you've seen me.'

I did not mind that. Disobedience is at least a healthy fault of childhood.

'Come along with me,' I said, 'and we'll confess everything to Mummy, and then I'll beg you off.'

He agreed to that cheerfully, safe in the feeling that he had one grown-up on his side, and stepped outside the shop with me.

'Since you've got plenty of money,' I said, 'why don't you buy some good sweets instead of that cheap trash?'

'I don't care much for them,' he admitted, 'I only bought them to get change.'

To get change!

'And where,' I added, 'did you get that golden sovereign, you young rascal.'

'Auntie Kate gave it to me,' he replied promptly.

I hadn't the least idea who Auntie Kate might be. Probably, I thought, some fictitious relation like myself, since I knew of no real one bearing that name. Then, suddenly, as if regretting his confidence, he clutched my arm.

'Don't tell Mummy about it, will you? And don't tell her I spoke about Auntie Kate. Don't tell her anything.'

In a weak moment I promised, and regretted my promise the moment after.

'You oughtn't to have secrets from your mother,' I said. 'And who is Auntie Kate, any way?'

'Oh,' he answered airily, with his monstrously grown-up air, 'she's a friend of mine, you know.'

'A friend of yours. Not of your mother's, too?'

'Oh, yes, of course.'

I could tell at once that he was lying.

'Tell me truthfully,' I said sternly, i know she's not your real Aunt. But does Mummy know her at all?'

'No, she—she doesn't.'

'Then why did you say she did?'

He turned a little sulky.

'I only-told you about her in case you thought I'd stolen the pound.'

Dick's little son a thief! That he should dream me capable of thinking it!

I stared at him aghast.

'Of course, I wouldn't steal,' he said uneasily. 'But, you know, some people would do anything for money. They'd take it with them when they died if they could.'

I could tell at once that he was quoting somebody.

'Did your Auntie Kate tell you that?' I asked.

'Yes.'

'Who is she, Leo?'

'I dunno. She's Auntie Kate. She told me to call her that. I don't like her much. She looks so funny. And she only talks to me at night. But she gives me golden sovereigns sometimes. This is the third. She's got lots of 'em, she says. It must be lovely to have lots.'

The boy's talk had so engrossed me that I had not heard the crisp toc-toc of a trotting pony on the road behind us. We had nearly reached the station when I heard Sylvia Franklin's voice sing out from behind—

'So here you are, George, my dear. So glad to see you, and so dreffly, dreffly sorry to be late. I had so many things to do. I see you've already met my large son. Leo, how dare you be in the village.'

I had turned on first hearing her voice, and there she was, smiling and waving her whip at me. At thirty-two she had still the face and figure of a young girl. The twelve years which had elapsed since I first knew her had changed me from a young man to grey middle age, and left her untouched. It was with an odd sensation of walking back into my youth that I went to the near wheel of the trap and took her hand.

When I entered the drawing-room after dinner, behind the maid with the coffee-cups, I found Mrs Millington—Sylvia's mother, who lived with her—playing soft sleepy music on the piano. Sylvia occupied one end of a great settee near the fire, and moved her skirt to make room for me.

'Come and sit down here, George,' she said. 'And do smoke. A cigar or a pipe, if you like.' Then she shook her head at the maid who was hovering over me with the tray. 'No, Tomlin, Colonel Crossfield doesn't take coffee. Ask cook to make just one cup of China tea.'

This was indeed making me at home. Queer—and nice—that she should remember my little weaknesses after so long. It occurred to me, not for the first time, that I might marry her, but I put the thought away from me. I had much affection for her, but not the love that had surprised and blinded me when I was a settled bachelor of thirty-eight. Now, as a still more settled bachelor of fifty, I was loth to change my state. Besides, I did not want the ghost of Dick Franklin for a rival. And again, because Dick was killed under my command, it might set ill-natured people whispering about David and Uriah. Oh, there were several reasons.

But I was very glad to be there, and it was with a sensation of perfect ease and harmony that I fumbled in the bulging pocket of my dinner-coat for my old pouch and pipe.

'How time flies!' Sylvia murmured. 'We've been here nearly two years. You haven't yet told me how you like the house.'

'It's charming,' I said. 'But isn't it—well—rather big for you.'

'It's dreadfully expensive,' she sighed, 'if that's what you mean.'

'Why not travel—live in hotels?' I suggested bluntly. 'You'd be having a good time and saving money.'

'I think a country home's best for the boy. I want him to feel that he belongs somewhere. And I hate being cooped up in a little place.'

All this seemed reasonable enough, and I inclined my head.

'It's nice to have you down here,' she added, 'I've been—wanting you.'

I was not such a fool as to misunderstand her.

'About something in particular?' I asked.

'Yes. It's no good, George. I don't understand boys. When Leo was born I thought he'd always have his father to look after him. But, you see'

She broke off suddenly, giving me a certain sense of satisfaction. I think I was glad that she, too, could see that there was something wrong about the boy. It confirmed my own judgment, and, moreover, it showed that maternal affection had not blinded her to any of Leo's less admirable traits.

'You're worried about him?' I asked.

She hesitated a moment, and then said very definitely, 'Yes'.

I determined to let her give me her confidence when and how she pleased.

To this end I purposely led her off at a tangent.

'That reminds me,' I said, 'I'd intended bringing something down with me for Leo. A pretty kind of uncle he'll think me. I must remedy that tomorrow.'

'For goodness' sake, don't give him money, then.'

'Why not?'

'Because'—she was laughing and trying to speak lightly—'because he's a most appalling little miser! I can't think from which side he can inherit that pleasant trait. But there it is.'

'How do you mean—a miser?'

'Just what I say. He doesn't spend money when he gets it. And he doesn't save it to any purpose that I can discover, like a reasonable child. He just hoards it! Somewhere—I don't know where—he's got a regular little miser's hoard. I've tried to make him open an account at the Post Office Bank, but he won't hear of it.'

'You're not firm enough with him,' I suggested,

'I know I'm not. But what can I do? I can't hit the child!'

No, Sylvia could not hit him. The idea of her raising a hand in anger was somehow ludicrous.

'I've get a queer feeling all the time,' she continued, 'as if Leo's under somebody else's influence. And I don't know who it could be.'

'He ought to be,' I said. 'You ought to send him away to a prep school.'

'Oh, George! He's all I've got, and he's very young yet, you know.'

'They take 'em even younger,' said I. it's hard on you, I know; but if you feel that the boy ought to have stronger handling. . . . And there's nothing more detestable in children than miserliness.'

'It's not only that. There's something else that I don't quite like. I know it's quite natural for girls to have imaginary friends. When I was small I had one myself, but I knew quite well that she was imaginary. But is that sort of thing right for boys?'

'I shouldn't think so. Why? Has Leo'

'Yes. It started eighteen months ago or more. He was always talking about her until I wouldn't let him. He tells me he doesn't see or talk to her now; we seldom mention her; but I know he still thinks he sees her. George, he's grown cunning!'

I was profoundly shocked. A thrill of a very unpleasant sort went through me. There was something tremendously unhealthy about all this.

'His imaginary friend is a she, then,' I said.

'Yes. He calls her Auntie Kate.'

'What!'

I exclaimed so loudly that Sylvia gave me a quick glance, startled and questioning.

'She's so imaginary,' I said, 'that she's given the boy a sovereign! Here it is!'

Truly, I had meant to keep Leo's secret. The betrayal of it was startled out of me before I had time to think. I saw a bright pink flush dye the cheeks of his mother.

'At least,' she said, i thought that he told the truth.'

I told her of my talk with him, and how I had unwittingly betrayed a confidence.

'Don't let the boy know I've told you,' I begged. 'He'll never trust me again.'

'He doesn't trust me!'

'But where could he have got it from. Look at the date. If this Auntie Kate gave it to him she can't be so very imaginary!'

'She is, George. Who can she be, then? He meets her in the house. And it's not one of the servants. I found that out a long while ago.'

Suddenly she caught my arm and gave it a little impulsive squeeze.

'George,' she said, 'I'm frightened. There's something terribly wrong with Leo. Help me!'

I gave her, of course, the same promise that I had given to Dick Franklin.

Next morning Leo was deputed to take me for a walk, that I might have further opportunity of studying him and gaining his confidence. I was quick to learn that he was not greedy after the usual fashion of young children. At the village shop, which we passed on our walk, they kept some quite reasonably good chocolates, but he declined my offer to get him some.

'I only like sweets just now and again, thank you, Uncle George.'

'What a funny chap you are! Suppose I were to give you half-a-crown, what would you do with it?'

He hesitated a moment,

'I should keep it.'

'Yes, but what would you spend it on? You'd spend it sooner or later, wouldn't you?'

'No, Uncle George.'

'Why not? What's the good of keeping it?'

'What's the good of spending it?'

'Well, you could buy a train, or some soldiers, or a compo cricket ball.'

'Yes, Uncle George. But I'd sooner have the money itself. . . . You see'

He faltered and broke off, and again I got an unpleasant little thrill. He was trying to find words to describe to me the miser's love of money for its own sake. As I didn't offer him the half-crown, he proceeded to angle for it.

'P'raps I'd change it, Uncle George, to make it look more.'

I didn't let him see how I despised this trait of his. The time for that was not yet.

'You've got a lot of money saved up, Leo?' I asked.

'Yes; but not as much as'

'Auntie Kate!'

'Oh, uncle, how did you guess?'

'Is she very rich?'

'I should fink so. You see, hers is all gold. And mine's all pennies and sixpences and shillings, to make it look more. She's promised to show me all her money one of these nights.'

'Not during the day, then?'

'No, Uncle George. She only comes at nights. But Mummy said I wasn't to talk about her.'

'You may to me. It's funny she won't come and see you in the daytime.'

'Oh, she's a queer one, Uncle George. I was frightened of her the first time she came. She's old and thin and ugly, Uncle George. But directly she comes I get sleepy, and you can't be afraid when you're really sleepy. She didn't come last night. It isn't every night.'

'What does she do, Leo? What a funny old woman!'

'Yes, isn't she. She just talks.'

'What about?'

'Money. She says it's the loveliest thing in the world, and the hardest thing to part from when they die for those who really love it. There's lots, she says, who would take it with them if they could, and they try to come back to it. She says it's better than love, food, drink, poetry, music, all the arts'

'For God's sake child!' I burst out in horror. The very tone was not his own. Children sometimes borrow inflections of the voices of others, and in his small piping accents I caught a note that made me shudder. It was like an unconscious parody of something vile.

He looked up quickly and innocently.

'Have I said something wrong, Uncle George. I beg pardon. I do say wrong things sometimes by accident. It's only what she says.'

'Leo,' I said gravely, i don't think Auntie Kate is quite nice, do you? I don't think you ought to know her.'

'That's what Mummy used to say. But I can't help it, Uncle George. I didn't want her to come at first.'

'And now you do?'

I could see that he did, but he tried to avoid admitting it.

'You see, she's given me free sovereigns altogether, Uncle George!'

'Leo,' I said gravely, 'when you are a little older you will understand how nasty it is to like money just for its own sake. Your father would be grieved if he knew—and perhaps he does know. Mummy's grieved, too. And you love Mummy more than Auntie Kate, don't you?'

'Ye-es,' he said; and I could see that his small mind had already given up the seemingly hopeless task of making a grown-up 'understand things'.

'Has Mummy ever seen Auntie Kate?' I asked.

'No. Auntie Kate won't stop. She goes when she hears anybody coming. She goes ever so quickly. Mummy came in once or twice, and told me not to talk to myself. And I wasn't!'

How shall I describe the ugly thoughts and half-thoughts that went drifting across my mind like blown smoke, when I can hardly describe them to myself. I had a feeling that I was snatching at something too horrible and grotesque to be real.

Before luncheon I had a little talk with Sylvia, and it was not about Leo.

'Who had the house before you bought it?' I asked.

She screwed up her brows.

'A man named—er—Rimple. Yes, that was it—Rimple. A funny old man he must have been. He was a recluse and a great scholar—Fellow of some college at Oxford. His sister, who was almost as queer from all accounts, used to keep house for him. She died first, and he followed within a month. . . . Well, and how did you get on with Leo?'

'Oh, we're very good pals. Still, I haven't the least idea what to get him. I suppose his godfather has seen that he wants for nothing.'

Now this was really a dig at Sylvia, for I had always been a little sore that I had not been allowed to stand godfather to the boy. I had supposed, when he first made his appearance in the world, that I should be his parents' first choice. Later, I had come to believe that his christening must have taken place while his father and I were on active service, but I was still a little sore that the ceremony had not been postponed until happier times.

'His godfather!' Sylvia exclaimed. 'My dear George, he hasn't got one!'

'Not got one!'

'Do you think you wouldn't have been asked? Oh, George, you'll think us all frightful heathens! You see he was bom such a little while before the war, and poor Dick had to go—and you too—so we put it off, hoping'

'You mean,' I said, 'that he hasn't been christened at all.'

She laughed like a naughty child.

'Isn't it dreadful!' she exclaimed. 'We really must get it done. You'll be one of the godfathers, won't you, George?'

No man ever hated the idea of spying more than I do. But necessity justifies most things—even that. That I, a retired colonel of the British Army, with an unsullied record so far as square, upright, manly dealing was concerned—that I should play the part of some despicable little mid-Victorian usher and spy upon a boy, was a thing I should have deemed impossible a short while before.

Leo, of course, went to bed early, but his mother and I went upstairs after dinner to say goodnight to him. Ever since he had been promoted to that stage of manliness which entailed the dismissal of his nurse, he had slept quite alone, and, having no fear of the dark, had never given any trouble on that account.

'I expect he'll be asleep,' said Sylvia. 'The soundness of his sleep has frightened me sometimes. You'd think he couldn't possibly have had any sleep the night before.'

But tonight Leo was awake, and, although he did not appear to be sleepy, he seemed disinclined to talk to us. He kissed us both, and we went downstairs again.

That night I made an excuse and retired early, but not to bed. I can honestly state that I was simply aghast at myself for what I caught myself believing—or, if I did not actually believe, I considered possible. I was taking seriously to account a child's delusions. I was going to wait up and see if I, too, saw and heard the impossible. Delusions? Well, the sovereign I had in my waistcoat pocket was real enough. And—I was going to spy on Dick Franklin's little son!

Opposite the boy's room was a bathroom, with a long rectangular unglazed window above the door. An eye practised in strategy had already seen the possibilities of this door. To this bathroom I went, after a brief visit to my own room, during which I exchanged my dinner-coat for an old golf jacket.

Leo slept with his door open, for the double purpose of supplying him with plenty of fresh air, and also that he might be heard if he had reason to call out in the night. His grandmother slept next door, but she was a sound sleeper and slightly deaf. Before finally retiring to the bathroom I took a peep at the boy. He was sound asleep.

Inside the bathroom I locked the door, to be on the safe side, although I had little fear of being disturbed that night. Then I carried a chair to the door and ascertained that by standing on it I could see through the small window above. I also discovered that the small window could be raised.

From my post on the chair I could see a little way into the boy's room through the half-open door. I could distinguish the neat little mahogany wardrobe and the bookcase full of children's volumes, but three-quarters of the room, including that part in which the bed lay, was hidden from me.

Within three-quarters of an hour the house had settled into a reposeful silence. I heard Sylvia and her mother come up to bed, the shutting and bolting of doors below, footfalls and subdued voices and laughter of maids on the back stairs; then all was quiet.

I don't know how long I kept that vigil, the strangest vigil of my life. I found that my watch had stopped, so that I had no means of judging the time.

After a while I was more than half persuaded that I was a fool for my pains, and half a dozen times I was on the point of giving up and retiring to my room. But the old habit of finishing what I had set out to do remained with me and I stayed on, growing more and more convinced that I had more imagination than sense.

When I was thoroughly cold and cramped and bored, I at last succumbed to the temptation to put on a pipe. Then, realising that I could hear the least sound through the open window above the door, I got down and sat on the chair on which I had been standing.

I am a slow smoker, and I was coming to the end of my pipe when I became aware of an intermittent sound, gentle and sibilant. I thought at first it was the hiss of damp tobacco in the bottom of my pipe, and stopped smoking to ascertain. In a moment I had found out that the sound had some other cause, and that it did not proceed from inside the room.

Stealthily I remounted the chair and looked out through the little window. I could see nothing but the half-open door of the boy's room, the dim outlines of furniture already described, the various shades of dusk. But I could hear something even more distinctly now, and my heart gave a sudden jump, as I recognised the almost unmistakable sound of voices whispering.

Stealthily, I got down from the chair again, and stealthily, with trembling hands, I lifted it away from the door. A minute later I was out in the passage and creeping across it towards Leo's room.

No longer was there any room for doubt. There was a voice whispering—a voice that was strange to me. It was growing louder, so that presently I was able to pick up words. An unctuous voice it was that whispered; soft, insinuating, nastily gleeful.

I halted a long minute on my toes outside the boy's room. I am not proud to have to confess it, but a great fear was on me, and I did not know how to force myself further. More distinctly than ever could I hear that whispering voice—

'Oh, the loveliness of them ... the little yellow discs ... the sweet gleam of them in the moonlight, child! Oh, to plunge one's hands among them and lift up great brimming palmfuls ... the music of their tinkling, coin upon coin. Oh, never lute nor violin made such music, child!'

Then, while I asked myself if I were mad, I heard Leo's voice for the first time. He whispered back drowsily, dreamily, as if in a kind of stupor, 'Oh, lovely, lovely, lovely!'

I fought down the panic in my blood, and, with a sudden cry, forced myself into the room. What I saw takes time to describe, but I saw it only for a moment.

Leo was lying quite still in bed, one cheek embedded in the pillow, and only his profile visible to me. Bending over him was the form of a woman which stood upright, and turned towards me as I burst in upon them. She was tall and thin and old, and wore some kind of tight-fitting dark gown over her broomstick figure. She wore a white collar—something like a boy's Eton collar—and white cuffs. Her eyes were large and hollow and staring, her skin yellowish and drawn tight between jaws and cheekbone. But my concern was with the boy, and it was he I stared at after that awful fraction of a moment.

'Leo!' I cried.

He gave a little start, uttered a cry, and sat bolt upright.

'Uncle George! Auntie Kate's here!'

But Auntie Kate was not. She was gone in the small fraction of time during which my eyes were off her.

'She comes and goes so quickly,' the boy murmured.

I daresay there are those who will think me a superstitious old fool. There are some, too, who do not know that a layman can perform the simple ceremony of christening. I don't know what I really believed, but it seemed to me that the placing the boy within the pale of Christianity might leave him less of a prey to the riff-raff of the spirit world, whose object is to bring wretched humanity to their own pass.

So I wetted my fingers in the ewer and touched the boy's forehead. . . .

Next day Leo left home with me and spent a jolly week in Brighton before going straight on to a prepatory school at Eastbourne. He had not been there a fortnight before he wrote home and confessed to his mother that he had a hoard of money buried under an elderberry tree in the kitchen garden. I dug it up in her presence. We found seven pounds ten in silver and copper interred in three old cigar boxes.

That was not the only hoard discovered in the grounds, for a month later Sylvia ordered the levelling of an old hollow tree, and in the hollow, cunningly concealed by leaves and bits of bark, was an old tin box which contained more than fourteen hundred sovereigns. The find made quite a stir in the neighbourhood, and public opinion attributed the hoard to Catherine Rimple, who had kept house for her hermit brother for many years. Her love of money had been a by-word in the neighbourhood.

That is almost, but not quite, all. I am not going to venture on any kind of explanation. I have my own theories and other people may have theirs. In support of my own I could instance the marked change in Leo when he came home for the holidays.

'Do you remember, Mummy,' he exclaimed on one occasion, 'when I was a kid I used to dream about a woman I called Auntie Kate. I used to think she gave me sovereigns sometimes, and told me to hide them up, and take them out and look at them when nobody was about. I wonder where I got the sovereigns from. I expect I just found 'em. Wasn't it funny?

As regards his altered character, let his last letter, written to me from the prep school at Eastbourne—where he is showing promise of becoming a stout cricketer—speak for itself:

'DEAR UNCLE GEORGE, Thanks so awfully for comeing to see me and giveing me that ten shillings. I'm afraid I blewd it all at the shop nex day, for the fellows were all round me becos they knew youd been to see me and I cant bare being stingy. But this isnt a hint for more becos tomorrow is pocket money day and I am also going into strict training for the sports so I must now close.

'With love from
LEO'.

The Lady of The Elms

But if he lives on for years and years, Maisie?'

The tall, slim girl who leant against the high mantelpiece looked into her lover's eyes with a pathetic little smile.

'He can't,' she answered. 'The doctors say it can only be weeks—months at most. Oh, Wilfred, dear, you know I can't leave him! If he lives another twenty years we shall have to wait. I do want to marry you, dear, but—but cross and crotchety and selfish as he is, I don't want him to die.'

'Selfish!' The young man seized upon the word. 'That's mild compared with what I should call him. He doesn't care a rap for you, but he insists on having you here because you can run the house and have the knack of being able to manage the servants. You promised when he adopted you that you would look after him as long as he lived, and he holds you to it in the face of—of'

Maisie Stanhope leant forward, still with the sad, sweet smile on her lips, and rubbed her knuckles against Wilfred Roper's smooth cheeks.

'A bargain is a bargain, you know,' she said. 'Remember, I should have been very badly off if he hadn't taken me in.'

The young man shrugged his shoulders impatiently.

'Yes,' he said. 'Well, I don't blame him so much for refusing to consent to our marriage. As you say, it wouldn't be playing the game to leave him, even if he were willing. But it's a damnable piece of tyranny to forbid me the house and to refuse his consent to our engagement. I suppose he thinks the roof over your head ought more than to recompense you for the splendid way you've looked after him. Come to think of it, why shouldn't he let us marry and live here? The house is big enough, goodness knows! And I've money enough to pay for our share of things.'

Maisie shook her head. She was more gentle and tolerant than her lover, who, in the first blush of an ardent and genuine love, was ready to revile every obstacle that stood in his way.

'Grandfather wouldn't hear of that,' she said simply.

'No, I know he wouldn't. He won't let us be engaged—wouldn't let me see you if he could help it—simply because he's afraid that I should get some of the attention that ought to belong to him. Girls in love, he argues, are thoughtless and aggravating. If you were in love the household wouldn't run so smoothly. Therefore you must not—shall not—think of being in love.'

The girl took a step forward, threw her arms impulsively around Roper's neck and kissed him.

'Don't go on grumbling, dear,' she begged, 'I know it's hard, but it's just as bad for me as it is for you. And don't think too badly of poor old grandfather. He's had a very unhappy life, and people like that are apt to be selfish when they have the chance to get everything their own way. After all, he suffers a lot, and hasn't long to live, whereas you and I have years and years in front of us in the ordinary course of nature.'

The young man drew her into his arms. His rather sulky lips lengthened into a pleasant smile, and his face lightened.

'Kiss me again,' he said, 'and for your sake I'll think he's everything that's kind and generous.'

She did as he asked, and then gave him a little push.

'Now, Wilfred, dear,' she said abruptly, 'I'm sorry, but I must turn you out. The housemaid will be back soon, and I don't trust her. She'd be as likely as not to tell grandfather, and if he knew I'd disobeyed him by letting you come here, it might upset him so much as to bring on another attack.'

Wilfred Roper laughed.

'This is about the queerest kind of courtship on record,' he said. 'The only nights I can come here are the housemaid's nights out. I wish you'd give her more leave, Maisie.'

Maisie laughed too.

'I can't give her more than two evenings a week,' she answered. 'It would spoil her, and, besides, she'd suspect something. Cook wouldn't say a word to anybody, I know. She's a dear.'

Roper moved towards the door, buttoning up his coat.

'Oh, well, I s'pose I'd better go, then!' he said. 'Good night, darling.'

Two minutes later Maisie let her lover out by the tradesmen's door. They had been talking in the breakfast-room, which was situated in the basement of the gloomy old-fashioned house; and the side door was very useful for surreptitious exits and entrances. The night was dark; a south wind wandered restlessly among the fruit trees in the walled-in garden, and a few drops of rain slanted down on to her face. She waved her hand as he reached the gate, and then drew back and closed the door.

The Elms, a huge, roomy old Queen Anne house, stood on the north side of a suburban common. The house and its great garden of fruit and flowers were screened from the eyes of the world in general by a wall that ran all around. On top of the wall broken bottles had been set in cement to discourage venturesome little boys.

Old Stanhope was dying of heart trouble, living from hour to hour in fear of the next attack, which would, as likely as not, close the gates of this world upon him. He was cantankerous, irritable, and selfish, and by no means reconciled to his approaching end. Human nature, particularly as applied to women, was, he held, of a very low order indeed. He had married twice, and his two wives, whom he had survived, had both given him a great deal of trouble and no return of his affection, and this perhaps accounted for his jaundiced outlook. He spent his days and evenings by the library fire, reading the Latin poets, ever ready to clutch at the bell-pull at the first symptom of a heart attack.

Maisie uttered a tired little sigh as she turned back into the breakfast-room. The house was her prison, and although she had a certain affection for it, its sadness always oppressed her. The subtle atmosphere of a past age hung over the place even when the windows were open to the sun and breeze of a summer morning. Something in the old-fashioned furniture, the pictures, the shapes of the rooms, reminded her of a sad little tinkling melody played in an old musical-box. Somehow it belonged to the Past and the people of the Past—the dull, stolid merchants and their families who had lived there in the days when Napoleon flung a grim shadow across the land.

The girl returned to the breakfast-room and placed a guard in front of the dying fire. It was almost time for her to go up and say good night to her grandfather, who might require her services in the decoction of a whisky nightcap. As she turned to the table to pick up her crochet-work she heard the library bell jangling violently in the kitchen, and afterwards the sound of a scraping chair as the cook got up to obey the summons.

Old Stanhope always rang the bell impatiently, as if resentful that his wants had not been attended to in advance, and Maisie had no reason to suppose that he had been taken ill. She listened without any anxiety to the cook's heavy footsteps on the stairs and in the hall above, until a shrill cry galvanised her into activity. She ran to the door and flung it open as the cook came pounding down the stairs. They met in the passage outside.

'Be quick, miss,' the woman gasped. 'He's been took bad again. And, oh, miss, the lady's there outside the door! Don't take no notice of her, miss.'

Maisie had no time to inquire who the lady was; indeed the cook's words made no impression upon her at the time. Without saying a word she ran up the basement stairs and turned into the hall.

The hall was long and narrow, and contained only one light, a gas-jet half turned up. There was a bright circle of light on the ceiling, but the floor and the lower extremities of the walls were dim in soft unwavering shadows.

There was dead silence about the place, save for the steady slumberous voice of an old grandfather clock.

Maisie, intent only on haste, had taken three or four steps from the basement stairs before perceiving that she was not alone in the hall. A female figure stood by the library door with an air of one waiting. The girl stared, uttered a little cry of surprise, and halted, throwing her arm out against the wall to steady herself.

The figure by the door stood quite motionless, and Maisie saw that it belonged to a girl as young as herself. But the intruder wore the fashion of the eighteen-sixties—a little round hat or bonnet, a white blouse cut after a somewhat severe pattern, rather short to meet a high waist, and a monstrous crinoline. In her left hand she carried a white parasol that looked ridiculously small. Maisie's first quick, frightened look took in all these details.

'Who are you?' she asked in a small dry voice.

The unknown visitor, the left side of whose profile was turned towards her, paid no heed and seemed not to have heard. Then it was that Maisie noticed another detail of her appearance. Her pale, fragile beauty was marred by an ugly red scar along the cheek-bone.

Maisie had time to think, for terror and thought come on swifter wings than light. She knew' that it was no living woman that stood by the library door; that her imagination had played some trick on her, or that a woman had come back from the grave wearing her earthly form.

To reach her grandfather, who stood in sore need of her, she had to pass this shadow, phantasy, or whatever it was; and for one terrible moment the task seemed impossible. In that moment she found herself weak and ill. Then she heard the heavy, reassuring tread of the cook on the basement stairs, and, closing her eyes, she made a rush for the library door, which had been left open. Not until she way half-way across the room did the frenzy leave her, and then she opened her eyes full upon her grandfather, the sight of whom dispelled all terror from her mind.

He sat in his usual chair before the fire, a Morocco-bound volume of Horace open at his feet. He was lying far back, and leaning over a little to the right, his face contorted, his hands clenched, his eyes open but apparently sightless. Evidently he had had time to pull the bell, but none to get at the little phial that he carried in his breast pocket.

Maisie ran to him and loosened his collar. Then she felt for the phial which the doctor had given him, found it, and set it to his lips. Presently he stirred, uttered a low moan, and the light of understanding came back into his eyes. The girl, shaking like a leaf in the wind, breathed a little sigh of relief.

'Are you better now, grandfather dear?' she asked.

'Better?' He stirred ponderously, as if afraid to move. 'Better? Oh, my God, a little better!'

Maisie turned and saw that the cook had entered the room behind her.

'Get the brandy,' she ordered abruptly.

The old man's bluish lips caught at the word.

'Yes, brandy. That was a near thing. I thought'

The cook had hastened to a cupboard. She now returned with a bottle and a glass, and administered a stiff dose of the neat spirit to the old man.

'That's better, sir,' she said. 'In about half-an-hour you'll be ready for us to help you upstairs. Shall I sit with you until then, sir?'

Old Stanhope nodded.

'Yes,' he said, 'you're stronger than Miss Maisie—in case'

Down in the basement a bell began to clamour. The housemaid had returned, and wanted to be let in. The cook glanced at Maisie, as if respectfully suggesting that she should go.

Maisie hesitated. Her fear returned to her with a sudden violence. She gazed at the cook with wide eyes, and the woman understood.

'It's all right, miss,' she said, 'she's gone now.'

'Who's gone?' mumbled old Stanhope.

Neither took any notice of the question, and Maisie, now reassured, went to the door. On the threshold she turned and looked back.

'Cook,' she said as evenly as she could, 'I wish you'd come to my room for a few minutes after the master has gone to bed. I have something to say to you.'

Maisie asked the cook to close her bedroom door, and invited her to take one of the armchairs; but the woman remained standing close to the door.

'Yes, miss?' she said.

'Who is she?' Maisie asked.

There was no need for her to put the question any more clearly. The cook knew very well who was meant by 'she'.

'Now bless you, miss,' she said, 'you're not to go and worry yourself over 'er. She can't do you any 'arm, poor thing. I 'oped you'd never see her, but there it was, you see. I couldn't 'elp it tonight. But don't you worry, miss, she couldn't 'urt anybody; she's only a shadow.'

'You've seen her before, then?' Maisie asked in a strained voice.

'Oh, yes, miss, several times! And a bad turn it gave me when I first seen her. Then I says to myself, "She can't 'urt you, and you may be like 'er yourself one of these days." She's all right, pore thing.'

'If you've seen her before, why haven't I?' Maisie demanded.

The cook hesitated.

'Well, miss, it's like this. You know I always answers the master's bell, in case he's took ill, that housemaid being such a fool? The last half-dozen times he's been took bad I've seen 'er standing outside the door. You've never seen her before, miss, because she's always been gone by the time you got upstairs. Poor thing, she looks very sad. I'm sorry for her, that I am!'

Maisie spoke in a strained but even voice.

'Why didn't you tell me about this before,' she asked.

'And having you getting frightened? Not if I knew it! She give me a turn the first time I seen her, but I reasoned with myself. I thought to myself, "If I tells Miss Maisie she won't believe me, an' she'll think I'm a fool, or she will believe me, and get frightened about it." I didn't want that to happen, miss.'

The girl smiled.

'All right, cook,' she said, i think you were very brave and good about it. I don't think I shall be so frightened if I see her again. But you won't tell Alice or the charwoman, will you?'

'Oh, no, miss, certainly not!'

Silence fell between them for a few minutes. The cook stood examining the tips of her red fingers, and Maisie stared into the empty grate, 'I wonder what she wants,' Maisie said presently.

'I think I know, miss.' The cook lowered her voice. 'She's come to fetch him. Every time he has an attack she's there, waiting. The time hasn't come yet, but when it does she'll be there, and ready.'

Maisie shivered.

'I wonder who she was,' she whispered,

'I expect the master would know, miss.'

'You won't tell him?'

'Why, no!'

There was another spell of silence, and presently Maisie looked up and said, 'That's all, cook. Thank you very much. I will say good night now. I want to think.'

The cook edged towards the door, her eyes still on her young mistress.

'Good night, miss. You're not going to be frightened.'

'No,' Maisie answered, i shall try not to be frightened.'

But for all that it took her a long while to drop off to sleep that night. She could not think without a shudder of that strange figure lingering outside her grandfather's door while he hovered on the brink of death. But it was a kind, sweet face, a good face, and from that she took some comfort. In the bright morning sunlight which greeted her when she awoke that outstanding event of the night before seemed to her like a grotesque dream.

All next day Old Stanhope was irritable and nervous, as he always was after a seizure. Late in the afternoon he sent for Maisie, who found him propped up in his chair, glaring into the fire that was always kept burning.

A handsome figure he looked in his old age, for all his wrinkles and pallor and the dark rings around his eyes. He had been very comely as a young man, and the remnants of these good looks remained in his high forehead, aquiline nose, and soft white hair. He did not look at Maisie until she stood close beside him, and then, as he moved his head and lifted his eyes, she saw that he was frowning.

'I want to know,' he said abruptly, 'who was in the house last night?'

Maisie, thinking of Roper, started, but her grandfather went on before she could answer. 'You know perfectly well,' he continued, 'that I don't want people here. I have had to tell you of that scores of times. And because I am an invalid, and unable to manage my own household, you take advantage of me. It is not a fair return for what I have done for you. I will not have people here, especially women.'

The girl stared at him in blank amazement.

'There were no other women here last night,' she said, 'except myself and the servants.'

The old man raised his eyebrows.

'My dear child,' he said, 'however much one may despise your charming sex one cannot be insulting to its members. If any man had made that statement to me I should have employed a certain epithet. As it is I must beg you to reconsider it.'

'There were no other women in the house last night,' Maisie repeated, trembling.

The old man clicked his tongue.

'Then pray whom was the cook referring to as you were making to go out of the room, when she said, "It's all right, miss, she's gone now"?'

Maisie did not answer, although the old man continued to fix inquiring eyes on her.

'And whom were you addressing outside the room before you came in? I heard you speak to somebody in an undertone. I was not quite unconscious. I heard you.'

'I—I don't know who it was,' Maisie faltered.

The old man raised his eyebrows. Cynical lines appeared at the comer of his mouth.

'You have perhaps forgotten her name?' he suggested drily.

Maisie hesitated. Something prompted her to lay bare the truth. She had determined never to tell him, and certainly it was no impulse to defend herself that prompted her. But suddenly she felt that he ought to know.

She bent and laid a hand on his shoulder.

if I tell you, will you promise not to be frightened, grandfather dear?' she said.

'I think I can promise as much as that, but I will not promise not to be angry. Who was it?'

'We don't know. It was a lady—quite a girl—who is sometimes seen in the hall. She wears a crinoline and very old-fashioned clothes. I have only seen her once, but cook's seen her several times.'

The old man's gaze fell away from her.

'A lady—a young girl—in a crinoline! Did you see her last night?'

'Yes, she was outside the door of this room. Cook says she is always there when you are taken ill.'

Old Stanhope's hands were shaking, but not with fear. Some other strong emotion had taken hold of him.

'What was she like?' he asked. 'Tell me.'

'She was about my height,' Maisie stammered, 'very pale and pretty, with small and cleanly-cut features. She wore a white bodice, a little round black hat, and carried a tiny white parasol.'

The old man leant forward, pressing his hands down upon his knees.

'Had she—a scar?' he asked with difficulty.

Maisie, bereft of words for the moment, could only nod.

'It was Stella,' the old man muttered. 'After all these years!'

There were tears in her eyes, and a moment later there were tears in Maisie's. Her hand, reaching out, fell lightly on his head.

'After all these years!' he repeated. 'And I thought no woman could love. I thought no woman had either soul or honour. But she, whom I had almost forgotten, remembers me. She remembers me even beyond this world!'

The old man looked up at her.

'My child,' he went on, speaking very slowly, 'I have had a life full of bitter experiences. It has made me turn from my own kind. But Stella remembers. If I had only known!

'She was a girl I loved when I was little more than a boy. We were on the point of becoming engaged when she died. I thought at the time that it had broken my heart. You said there was a scar on her face? I did that by an accident; and although it marred her beauty she said not one cross word to me, and would not hear me blame myself.

'Well—she died. Afterwards I married, and met with—with disappointments. I thought all women heartless and grasping, and looking back on Stella, I did her the injustice to suppose that she was, at heart, like all the others. And now it's a strange thing,' he went on, after a little pause, 'I remember telling her once that I was afraid of dying by myself. I envied those killed in battle for having comrades to go with them into the world beyond. She remembers that, Maisie, and that is why she waits outside the door when my time seems near. When the time comes she will take me by the hand, and I shall go with her without fear. Oh, thank God love is not a lie! I have lived in a nightmare for years. Maisie!'

'Yes, grandfather?' she answered in a little choked voice.

'You can leave me now. I want to enjoy my new' dream, which is really an awakening. But wait a moment. Wasn't there some young man who couldn't live without you—or so he said?'

'You mean Wilfred?' she asked in a low voice.

'Yes, that was his name. I told you I wouldn't have him here. Well, I suppose you'd only have waited for me to die, and then married him, in any case. Stella would say I was wrong about that. You'd better ask him here tomorrow. I should like to see him and shake hands with him. Now leave me for a little, and be happy, as I shall be!'

And Maisie went, stumbling for the tears that blinded her.

But it so chanced that old Stanhope never met Wilfred Roper.

Late that evening the library bell clamoured loudly in the kitchen, and Maisie, who heard it, fled upstairs to see what her grandfather required. As she entered the hall she saw two figures emerging from the library.

One was of the pale scarred girl in the crinoline, and she led by the hand a young man dressed in the fashion of the same period. He was tall, handsome, and well-proportioned, and there was something familiar to Maisie in his features.

It did not strike her until a moment or two later that this young man was exactly like what her grandfather might once have been. They were both smiling, and the light of love was in their eyes.

As they stepped out into the hall the shadows seemed to engulf them, and suddenly Maisie found herself staring at empty space.

She hurried forward and into the library. Her grandfather lay far back in his chair before the fire. He had just ceased breathing. His tired, lined face wore the look of a man who had died peacefully.

We end this volume with two pieces of non-fiction by AM Burrage.

The Supernatural in Fiction

I am continually being asked to recommend stories of the eerie sort. Nine people in ten seem to enjoy a good ghost story; and I have often thought that there must be more demand for such than the publishers know. Titles of books are often ambiguous, and the reader, anxious to set his flesh a-creeping, puzzles in vain over the catalogues. Those who would go frightened to bed know not where to purchase that peculiar and delightful fear. It is for the purpose of recommending a few such books that this article is written.

I myself am passionately fond of a good 'creepy' story, and have nibbled at more books than I can remember in the hope of finding the right food. Those stories which rank as classics need be no more than mentioned, for the very good reason that they are already so widely known. We have all read Scott's 'Tapestried Chamber', and 'Wandering Wullie's Tale' in Redgauntlet—both of which might have lost nothing by being a little shorter.

Most people discover early, and delight in, the sombre genius of Edgar Allan Poe. Stevenson's great masterpieces 'Markheim' and 'Thrawn Janet', both to be found in a volume entitled The Merry Men, are only a little less widely known. Ninety-nine people in a hundred have read and been thrilled by Mr W.W. Jacobs's 'The Toll House' and 'The Monkey's Paw'.

These are stories which everybody reads first, and, having read, searches the library shelves for more. And here I should like to intrude for the purpose of pointing out a book or two.

Dracula, by the late Bram Stoker, is the next to be mentioned, because of its vivid horror and the immense popularity which has been accorded to it. It is far from being a convincing book, and there are many artificialities and crudities in it to scratch the literary sense, but for all that it remains a monument of ghastliness, and those who have not read it should make a note of its title.

Mr E.F. Benson and Mr Barry Pain must both have been the cause of a number of people submerging themselves beneath the blankets o' nights. I was a boy when I read the latter's Tales Told in the Dark, and as I lay in bed after reading them, waiting for some nameless horror to creep out of the darkness to my side, I was not at all grateful to Mr Pain for his excursions into the unknown. One of these stories in particular, 'The Undying Thing', is all that a story of that kind ought to be. If the volume is now out of print, the pick of the author's earlier short stories have lately been collected, and many 'Tales Told in the Dark' are probably to be found between these new covers.

Mr E.F. Benson has written many ghost stories, and, since he could not tell a story badly if he tried, these eerie tales of his are to be specially recommended. The Room in the Tower is a volume of them which must have created quite a boom in night-lights. The first story, from which the book takes its name, is a triumph of creepiness, and most of the others are at least nearly as good.

The late Mrs Molesworth wrote some Uncanny Tales—one of her books bears that title—in the quiet but rather pleasant fashion of her day. This book is still to be found in circulating libraries and is well worth reading. Poe is not the only writer of supernatural horrors whom the Americans can claim as their own. The late Ambrose Bierce, another trans-Atlantic author, was his very worthy disciple. One of his books entitled Can Such Things Be? evokes the answer, i hope to goodness not!' After reading this collection of stories I kept the electric light up in my bedroom most of the night. It was not that I was afraid of anything, but I objected to the furniture creaking.

The name Algernon Blackwood is well known to all readers of ghostly stories. He can thrill us with the best when he likes, but he does not always like, for he will have little to do with the old-fashioned 'spook'. He finds his ghosts in unconventional places. They are hidden forces, secretly working good or ill, rather than visible spectres. But every book with his name on the cover has originality in it, and the reading of it is an adventure.

Some while ago two really admirable books of ghost stories appeared on the market, with a year or two between them. They were both from the pen of Dr James, a Cambridge professor. The first to appear, Ghost Stories of an Antiquary, was slightly the better, and contained 'Oh Whistle and I'll Come to You'—a real gem. Dr James offered no theories about his spectres. There is no modem jargon in his stories about 'auras' or 'the astral plane'. He set himself to the task of telling some real old-fashioned creepy ghost tales, and he succeeded to admiration. His second book, More Ghost Stories of an Antiquary, made a very worthy companion to the first.

Mr Oliver Onions is the author of another book which I have felt it my duty to recommend to most people of my acquaintance. There is some hair-raising stuff in Widdershins, particularly in the first story, which is also the longest. To give a misused word its right meaning for once, this is really an 'awful' story. There is great literary excellence in this book, besides satisfaction for the mere seeker after thrills.

Many humorous writers, seeking for a change from humour, have written good ghost stories. We have already dealt with Mr W.W. Jacobs and Mr Barry Pain. Mr F. Anstey is another. Years ago he wrote an excellent ghost story which is now to be found in a volume entitled The Talking Horse. One picks out ghost stories from among the work of many writers as a prospector for gold may find an occasional 'pocket'. It is rare indeed to discover a rich seam. But in the long row of books written by Sir Arthur Quiller-Couch there is a veritable mine of such stories, still perhaps awaiting the discovery of a few fortunate people—fortunate because they have yet to read them for the first time.

'Q' as a short-story writer has reached an unassailable position in English literature. He has most of Stevenson's delightful artistry and a great deal of his own. While he has written half a dozen stories at least as good as Stevenson's best, the total number he has written is amazing in view of their high level of excellence. There must be at least a dozen of his volumes of short stories on the library lists, and nearly all of them contain a ghost or two. Old Fires and Profitable Ghosts is the quaint title of one of these books.

In it are to be found many tales of a most engaging creepiness, notably 'The Seventh Man', which I defy anybody to read once without wanting to return to it.

Among some good ghost stories in Wandering Heath is one which I dare risk saying is almost the finest short story in the language. This is 'The Roll Call of the Reef', also to be found in Tales of Our Coast. I am not going to attempt to describe this exquisite little story. It remains to be read. Another little gem among ghost stories fashioned by 'Q' is 'Lieutenant Lapenotiere' in a more recent book entitled News From the Duchy. Other books by the same author in which ghosts are to be encountered are The White Wolf The Laird's Luck, I Saw Three Ships, and (if memory serves me) The Merry Garden.

I cannot lay sufficient stress upon the excellence of all these volumes.

Those who have yet to make their acquaintance should not delay an hour in seeking them out.

The late Henry James wrote a lot of stories which must be labelled uncanny. 'The Great Good Place' and 'The Figure in the Carpet' are two which propound the most teasing problems. But in 'The Turn of the Screw' he has written a tale at which one can only gasp. For sheer horror—and he keeps tightening the screw as we read on—this tale has never been equalled, and I dare to say that it will never be bettered.

It is a long story, one of two in a book entitled The Two Magics, and if the style presents difficulties to the reader who would hasten through it without pausing to think, it is a style admirably suited to such a story. What the author tells us in plain English is horrible enough. It is what he leaves unexpressed which is more horrible still. He opens up little avenues of thought, pushes us, and sets us wandering down them to go alone to the edge of places into which we dare not look.

It is only fair to state that this book should not be read by very young or neurotic people. The sceptic with the hardest nerves will not go comfortably to bed after having read it. To most of my acquaintances it has been a fearful joy. If Henry James had written nothing else he would still be one of the great writers of his time.

There are many other 'creepy' books well worth the reading, to which I shall perhaps refer on some future occasion.

Un-Paying Guests

For some reason, as yet undiscovered, ghost stories are more popular at Christmas than at any other time. Not only the ardent believers, but the sceptics and even the Sadducees seem to enjoy them. Stories of the occult are printed in periodicals which would never think of offering them to their readers at any other season of the year. Ghost stories are asked for and told by word of mouth around the fireside; and even the newspapers provide stories for their readers which they offer up as the truth. It is a poorly edited news-sheet that cannot find a ghost for Christmas.

Perhaps it is because at Christmas all we who have waved farewell to our childhood years ago try once again to be nervous happy little people, easily scared, and with an abnormal gift of faith. What healthy, old-fashioned child has not shivered beside the hot fender before bedtime, while nurse or mother told some story of goblins or witchcraft. We used to love Andersen and Grimm, but they used to frighten us. That was part, if not most, of their charm.

I suppose in time Science will definitely lay down the law about ghosts. I am glad that it will be after my day. It would be dreadful to have children either frankly incredulous, or speaking of psychic phenomena with the same smattering of scientific knowledge as now they speak about the rainbow or the front door electric bell. The ghosts which pseudo-scientific mediums are 'producing' are sad dull things, without a blood-curdling shriek or a flutter of the shroud in their compositions. I defy anybody to raise a thrill over the account of how some trussed-up charlatan, by the alleged aid of the departed, managed to remove his braces or throw a tambourine over a screen. No, when we get round the Christmas fire and become children again we want the real ghost story, the one with that spice of horror in it which brings the authentic thrill. The effect of these stories depends so largely upon the histrionic powers of the narrator—to be effective they must be told not written—that I do not hope to infuse them with the right amount of awesomeness. That is for the reader to do when he or she comes to re-tell them.

Some of you, this Christmas, will find yourselves around a great log fire in an oak panelled hall, the very time and place for ghost stories. Somebody will say as much before very long, and out will go the lights, and everybody will urge everybody else to begin. You will find yourselves shutting in the light of the fire, but in the penumbra behind you, stray gleams will focus upon the polished oak. Even while everybody is talking you will have but to look over your shoulder at the moving shadows, through which, perhaps, some old portrait may be frowning down, to catch the right atmosphere. You will see everybody drawing closer together and the circle narrowing. Well, here are some stories to tell around the Christmas fire. I have selected them from the many I have heard because all of them have been told me as true, and there are some which, even if I tried, I should find it very hard to disbelieve.

A friend of mine went to see some people who had just moved into a house at Hampstead. He arrived after dinner on a summer evening, and found the front door open. It was just dusk.

Opposite him at the far end of the hall he could see a maidservant with her back towards him standing motionless. Thinking she must have heard his approach he did not at once ring the bell, but as she took no notice he pressed the button, and heard it ring in the kitchen.

The servant neither moved nor spoke, but stood upright and in the same attitude as that in which he had first seen her. Then, as his eye got used to the gloom he saw that she was holding something to her left ear.

Then he understood. She was in the act of telephoning. The attitude was unmistakable. Doubtless she had been sent to get a call and could not leave the instrument until it came through.

He pressed the bell again, hoping that some other maid would hear and answer it, and in the act of doing so he took his eyes off the girl at the telephone. Immediately the drawing-room door opened and his host appeared.

As he was conducted into the drawing-room he saw that the maid was no longer in the place where he had seen her, but thought nothing more of it.

'Hope you haven't been waiting outside very long,' said his friend. 'The parlour-maid's out for the evening and cook's nearly stone deaf, so I had to keep my ears open for the bell.'

It did not occur to him then how curious it was that a stone-deaf cook should be using the telephone; but later, when asking his friend's wife how she liked her new house, he said, 'I see you've got the telephone here.'

His friend shook his head. 'No,' said he, 'there was one here when we arrived, but we had no use for it and had it taken away.'

'Why,' he exclaimed, 'while I was waiting at the door I could have sworn I saw one of your maids in the act of telephoning.'

They both laughed and assured him that there was no telephone in the house, nor was there at that particular time a servant in the house capable of using one. My friend was so surprised at this information that he went with them out into the hall and pointed to the exact spot where he had seen the maid standing. What made it stranger still was that it was from that very spot that the telephone had been removed.

A few days later the new tenants of the house heard of a tragedy which had occurred there in the days of its former occupants. A housemaid, who had been rung up to be informed of the death of her father, had dropped down dead from the shock.

A clergyman I used to know once told me a curious story about the wife and daughter of a dean, living within the precincts of a certain cathedral. He heard the story from their lips.

On a certain winter evening the two ladies were sitting in the drawing-room alone with their two dogs. Suddenly the dogs, for no apparent cause, exhibited signs of restlessness and anger, then of fear. While the younger lady was trying to quiet them the door opened, seemingly of its own accord. Nobody entered and nobody was standing outside, for, as the door opened, she could see out into the hall. At this the fear and fury of the two dogs reached a paroxysm, and it was some while before they could be got to lie down quietly again.

The two ladies were in the midst of discussing this strange and very unusual happening, when the elder said, 'What's that lying there on the floor?'

She pointed to a piece of paper which lay on the carpet in the middle of the room. The younger crossed over and picked it up. On it was written in angular but very beautiful characters, 'Je ne suis pas un diable. '

That is all. No explanation has since occurred to them. Nothing like it had ever happened to them before, nor was anything of the kind repeated up to the time when I heard the story.

I once heard a ghost story about a certain well-known actor who subsequently met his death in the war, although then he was well over military age. By something of a coincidence I met him shortly after having heard the story, and though I came to know him quite well I never cared to question him about it.

It seems that when he was a very little boy, living in a Scotch town, he used to speak to his mother and nurse about an old lady who used to wander about his nursery, and who was invisible to all save himself. His parents were at first alarmed deeming such an imagining to be unhealthy, but they knew such things were not uncommon with children, and, as the little boy seemed more pleased than otherwise to see his strange visitor, they took little notice. I may add that they did not believe in ghosts.

The boy used to describe the old woman as having a very kind face, and she used to smile at him and nod at him and encourage him to play. Now comes the sequel. One night the family were sitting at dinner, when from the top of the house there came a scream, followed by a crash. They rushed up to find that the little boy had fallen downstairs and lay unconscious on the landing below the nursery. When he was brought to, he said that he had jumped downstairs because the old lady had spoken to him; but nothing would induce him to divulge what she had said.

Enquiries soon brought to light a rather vague legend that that particular room was supposed to be haunted by an old woman; and the family made haste to move.

The little boy, when he grew up, would never tell this story, but he was willing to admit it under pressure. But he never told a soul what the old woman said to him, and the secret now lies buried with him under a wooden cross. Perhaps—who knows?—she told him about the scarred slope of Hill 60 and a predestined shell.

It is, within my own experience, a fact that certain people have been able to foretell the hour of their own death. There was a certain officer who joined my battalion in France from the reserve battalion at home sometime early in '17. He was a young and fit man who had caused some adverse criticism by managing to avoid being sent out before, although he had joined the army at the outbreak of war. The rumour that he knew he was going to be killed was quite freely discussed.

Everybody expected him to shape poorly as a soldier, but during those early and terrible days of March, when, fighting incessantly, we were driven without rest or respite across the Somme, he showed the highest possible courage. When, near Albert, the enemy paused and gave us our chance, and we turned to counter-attack, he was the only officer left in his company, and he had had sufficient hair-breadth escapes to imbue most men with false confidence.

On that morning, when the order came to advance, he wished his men luck, adding, 'I don't know what is going to happen now. I shall not be with you to see you through.'

He was killed an hour later, leading his men across a ploughed field.

Obviously he knew exactly when he was going to die, and that fact begs the question—Who told him?

My father, who always stoutly refused to believe in ghosts, used to tell a story which he was quite unable to explain. In the early 'seventies he had a friend whom I will call A, who in turn had a friend whom I will call W. W was an artist in black-and-white and also in oils. My father knew him, but not so intimately as he knew A, from whom he had this story.

W was a strange fellow with a German name, one of the finest illustrators of his day, and noticeably eccentric even among Bohemians. He had a studio at the top of an old house in the City, and lodgings in some outlying suburb.

The rest of this City house was let out in blocks of offices. It was deserted at night save for W, who occasionally slept there when he was indulging in a feverish spell of work.

There came a time when W's eccentricities increased to an extent which alarmed A. The artist was drinking very heavily at the time, but his general behaviour seemed to point to insanity. He was then trying to work very hard. He had, I think, some ambitious picture to finish in time to submit it for exhibition. He worked at that most of the day, and sat up at night doing black-and-white work for a religious magazine. This meant that he was sleeping at the studio.

One night A found him and took him to task about his behaviour, roundly accusing him of having something on his mind, and demanding confidence. W admitted that something was wrong with him, but could not be got to give the least hint as to the trouble. At last he said:

'Come back and sleep at the studio. There are two camp beds there. I don't feel that I can tell you anything tonight, but perhaps I shall feel more equal to it in the morning.'

A, being only too anxious to be of use to his friend, acceded to this strange request, and together they went to the deserted old house in the City, and climbed the stairs to the studio at the top. They sat talking for a short while, and then retired to bed.

A fell asleep almost at once, and was awakened sometime in the small hours by a sound below. As he lay listening he heard the chain fall from the street door and hurried footfalls cross the passage to the stairs and begin to mount them. The house was several stories high, but on the bare floors and stairs the footfalls were distinctly audible. Wondering who could be about the house at such a time, and obviously in a hurry, he lay straining his ears.

The footfalls mounted flight after flight of stairs, coming nearer and nearer, until at least they reached the top landing. They crossed the landing, the studio door burst open, and a man, dressed in the costume of the early Stuart period, burst into the room, flourishing a drawn sword.

A uttered a cry and sprang out of bed, only to find himself alone in the room with W who was sound asleep. Marvelling at what he thought to be a strange dream, A returned to bed, and presently slept again.

Next morning W seemed more cheerful, remarking that he had had his first proper night's sleep for some long while, adding that his friend's presence seemed to have done him good, and asking A rather pointedly what sort of a night he had had.

At first A intended telling his friend nothing of his strange experience, deeming him in too nervous a state; but W was so strangely insistent in asking him how he had slept that A, suddenly suspecting something, told his strange story.

W's face cleared at once.

'Well,' he said, when he had heard all, 'thank Heaven I'm not mad. It was that thought which has been troubling me. I'd been seeing that cavalier of yours every night for the last fortnight, and now you've seen him too, he must exist outside my own imagination. I shan't sleep here anymore.'

W, I believe, was as good as his word. Although both he and A tried hard to find out if any particular history were attached to the house, they were unsuccessful. It has given place since, to a new and probably unhaunted building, and its mystery will forever remain a mystery.

Early this year when I was in a rural district with a certain war correspondent whose name is well-known to everybody, we found ourselves near an old manor house with perhaps the worst reputation for hauntings of any house in the British Isles.

The family had lived in it for generations, but had shut it up entirely a few years ago, and moved into a more modem and smaller house on the same estate. They had done this for no apparent reason, and the picturesque old house is now crumbling into decay. Many terrifying stories are told about the happenings in this old house o' nights. Not a few have attempted to drive the ghost away, but they have been only too glad to effect their own escape and leave the ghost in possession. Certainly there is one well-known Catholic priest whom nothing would induce to spend another night there.

Being desirous of seeing the ghost for ourselves we called on the lady who now lives in the smaller house. Probably my friend's name was well-known to her, for she received us very graciously until we mentioned our errand. Then her expression changed altogether. She looked angry and frightened as if we had offered her an insult.

'We never speak about that house,' she said; and that was all we could get out of her. She would not even hear of our going over it in daytime. I must confess that my curiosity is sadly piqued because of that old house. One may be a sceptic of the sceptics, but it is not for nothing that a family leaves a house which has been its home for three hundred years. Ghost or no ghost, whatever that house contains has frightened the people who own it; but there the mystery remains for the present.

As a very young man I once stopped at a South Coast boarding house for a short while during the winter. I had not been there long when my plans changed, and I thought of moving on to some other place. I mentioned this to the proprietress, who looked at me rather strangely, and afterwards took me aside and asked me if I had seen anything.

I did not understand her, and said so, but she seemed not to believe me.

She said that if I had, there was nothing to be afraid of.

Mystified, I began to ask questions, when she told me that the house, which had once been a convent, was haunted by a nun. She, her daughters, and all the permanent guests had seen her several times; in fact so often that they were scarcely nervous of her.

'She never does any harm,' said the good lady, 'and so long as I don't have to pass her on the stairs I don't mind.'

Later, in the drawing-room, in the absence of all temporary visitors save myself, they spoke quite openly of this un-paying guest, and I heard the various experiences of daughters and boarders. I thought at first that I was the victim of a rather elaborate joke, but there were so many there to whom joking would have been entirely foreign that I had to believe. They had all seen the nun about the house, generally on the stairs or in the hall, and had ceased to be unduly perturbed at the sight of her.

I must confess, however, that although I remained a few days longer I never saw her.

As the writer of a great many stories about ghosts I am often asked if I believe in such things; but I seldom commit myself. When asked if I have ever seen a ghost I have to answer that I don't know. Certainly I once had a very strange experience; but that is a story which I am not going to tell.

A.M. Burrage – The Life And Times.

Alfred McLelland Burrage, better known as simply AM Burrage, was born in Hillingdon, Middlesex on July 1st, 1889, to Alfred Sherrington Burrage and Mary E. Burrage. On his Father's side writing already ran in the family's blood as both he and an uncle, Edwin Harcourt Burrage, were writers of the then very popular boys' magazine fiction.

Life in late Victorian times was by no means easy and writing has always been a precarious career for most. For an insight into the young AM and his surroundings it is interesting to see how certain facts were captured in the 1891 census when he was aged one. The family is listed as living at Uxbridge Common in Hillingdon. His father is 40 and his mother 36. In the next census of 1901, and with it the end of the Victorian era, the family has moved to 1 Park Villa, Newbury. In that time his father has aged 17 years his mother 6 years and young AM has disappeared from the records. It's almost a precursor to one of his stories.

There is little documented about his growing up and education. What we can glean though is something about his environment. His neighbours were varied: a tailor's journeyman, a corn porter, a lodging-house keeper and a grocer's assistant. Nothing particularly illustrious, so times cannot have been as rosy as they should, especially in the light of his Father's hard work. Alfred Sherrington wrote for The Boy's World, Our Boys' Paper, The Boys of England, and various others. He also appears to have written under the pseudonym Philander Jackson and edited The Boys' Standard and that one of his more celebrated pieces was a retelling of the story of Sweeney Todd entitled "The String of Peals; or, Passages from the Life of Sweeney Todd, the Demon Barber".

Sadly Alfred Sherrington Burrage died in 1906. There is a biographical note in Lloyd's Magazine, from 1921, which suggests that young Alfred McLelland was studying at St. Augustine's, the Catholic Foundation School in Ramsgate, and most probably away from home at the time.

A.M. Burrage was 16 years old when he had his first story published; the same year as his father's death, in the prestigious boys' paper, Chums. It was a great start to his professional career and whether doors had been opened by his father and family or not the young man's career now had to stand on its own. He was now primary provider for the household and this was the only way he could do it. His Mother, sister and aunt must be provided for.

Magazine fiction was his family's blood and business and for A. M. Burrage, business was good. He established himself as a competent and creative writer and was busy writing stories and articles on a weekly basis for publications such as Boys' Friend Weekly, Boys' Herald, Comic Life, Vanguard, Dreadnought, Triumph Library Cheer Boys Cheer, and Gem, under the pseudonym 'Cooee'.

However, unlike his father and uncle who had remained firmly and easily categorised as boys' writers, he had his sights set on the more well regarded, more lucrative, adult market. Burrage was aided in his early years as a professional writer by Isobel Thorne of the off-Fleet Street publishing firm Shurey's. Her publications have been characterised as "low in price, modest in payments, but whose readers were avid for romance, thrills, sensation, strong characterisation and neat plotting", and this estimation of her publications also fits nicely the description of Burrage's own writing at that time. For a young writer this sort of readership was vital, and the modest wages he received were bolstered by the exposure the publications brought him. Burrage was certainly helped by Thorne's use of young writers.

At the time Burrage was beginning to really establish himself as a writer, the entire magazine fiction scene was benefiting from what we would now see as disruptive influences: new printing techniques, a growing readership with more disposable income and leisure time and other media failing to provide – though obviously movies and such were only in their infancy at the time. The market was lively and commercial, and the readership interested, excitable and willing to pay. P. G. Wodehouse, of Jeeves fame, recalls these years:

We might get turned down by the Strand, but there was always the hope of landing with Nash's, the Story-teller, the London, the Royal, the Red, the Yellow, Cassell's, the New, the Novel, the Grand, the Pall Mall, and the Windsor, not to mention Blackwood's, Cornhill, Chambers's and probably about a dozen more I've forgotten.

With War clouds darkening the skies of Europe in 1914 Burrage was firmly established as a magazine writer, securing publication in London Magazine and The Storyteller, which were both highly prestigious publications. Alongside he had plenty printed in less illustrious publications such as Short Stories Illustrated.

By now Burrage, a young man of twenty-four-year-was eligible for the Armed Services. Under the 'Derby Scheme' he confirmed that he was available for service if called upon in December 1915. Conscription was to follow shortly though, by that time, Burrage had already voluntarily enrolled in the Artists Rifles.

The significance of Burrage's decision to join the Artists Rifles is made clear by the nature of the unit itself. They formed in the middle of the nineteenth century, a group of volunteer artists comprising musicians, writers, painters and engravers. Minerva and Mars were their patrons, one of wisdom, arts, and defence, the other of war. The unit boasted several significant figures as ex-servicemen, including Dante Gabriel Rossetti, Algernon Charles Swinburne and William Morris. It was a popular unit with students and recent postgraduates, and the training was considered and extensive.

In Burrage's vivid, celebrated account of World War I entitled War is War, he insists that he was a volunteer and not a conscript, though as has already been noted, it is quite possible that his decision to join such a respected territorial unit may have been more of an effort to secure himself a more congenial army posting; had he waited for conscription, he would have had little choice over those with whom he was posted. Unlike poets Wilfred Owen or Edward Thomas, Burrage did not achieve a commission, and he suggests in War is War that this may be a result of his extremely unmilitary personality and his shortcomings as a soldier.

Add to this the fact that as the breadwinner for the family he was putting himself in harm's way. If anything were to happen to him the result on the family would be devastating. With the death of
Edwin Harcourt Burrage in 1916 it came even more starkly into focus.

Even though he was now a soldier he was still a writer and writers had to write. It also helped that it was a distraction from the mindless carnage around him. He experimented with various genres, excelling in the one that was to prove most lucrative for him; the light romance, in which a male character invariably meets a female character, there is a problem or hurdle to their being together, they overcome it and they live happily ever after. Burrage's talent for this formula was such that he could work seemingly endless minor variations from the same basic storyline and so he was able to keep writing a steady body of easy work.

He gives a fascinating account of the practicalities of writing such fiction during wartime in War is War, in which he remarks on the difficulties of censorship: "the problem of censorship was an acute one to me. It was well enough to write a story, but the difficulty was to get it censored. Officers were shy of tackling five thousand words or so, written in indelible pencil..." After some time he managed to find a chaplain who was willing to undertake the censorship. However, in order to secure this chaplain's favour and thus his services he was obliged to appear to be holy. Though he did so in earnest while he was with the chaplain, his efforts were dashed when the chaplain found him, sprawled on top of a young girl, and realised Burrage's piety to be a fraudulent con. As Burrage had anticipated, the reality of his behaviour ensured that this particular opportunity was swiftly ended. Resourceful to the last, though, he writes of his solution: "there were 'green envelopes' which could be sent away sealed and were liable only to censorship at the base, but these were only sparingly issued... I met an A.S.C. lorry driver who had stolen enough green envelopes to last me for the rest of the war; and since he only wanted two francs for them I was free of the censorship from that day forward."

Although we know that Burrage had his family to support at home as an incentive to keep writing, at times in War is War he reveals a more intimate aspect of his relationship with his work.

"It was a great relief to me to write when it was at all possible – to sit down and lose myself in that pleasant old world I used to know and pretend to myself that there never had been a war. Some of my editors seemed of the opinion that we were not suffering from one now. One used to write to me saying "Couldn't you let me have one of your light, charming love stories of country house life by next Thursday." I would get these letters in the trenches during the usual 'morning hate' when my fingers were too numb to hold a pencil, when I was worn out with work and sleeplessness, and when I was extremely doubtful if there ever would be another Thursday".

Writing is a useful therapy and for Burrage it provided a means to escape if only for a short time to a world that he could control and move at will. With the misery and harsh conditions of the War dragging on he was eventually invalided and so he returned to England.

One of the best insights we have as to the character which Burrage presented on his return from the war is to be found in Lloyd's's 1920 publication of Captain Dorry, one of Burrage's story series. In that publication there was included a brief sketch of Burrage, describing his personality.

A.M. BURRAGE is the type of young man who might very well walk out of one of his own stories. He commenced yarn-spinning as a boy of fifteen at St Augustine's, Ramsgate, writing stories of school life to provide himself with pocket-money. Since then he has won his spurs as one of the most popular of magazine writers. Everything he does has charm and reflects his own romantic spirit – for he is incurably romantic and hopelessly lazy. It is his misfortune, although he would not admit it, that his work finds a too ready market. Nevertheless, his friends hope that one day he will wake up and do justice to himself. Otherwise he may end up as a "best-seller", a fate which doubtless he contemplates with equanimity.

Despite the sketch's fairly accurate but negative summation of Burrage's literary output up to that point, some of his stories seem to exhibit a desire to write about more than just his usual romantic plots. The most immediate change of this nature is in his decision to bring some of his wartime experience into his work, despite being perfectly aware that such writing was not at all what his editors desired, for they feared it would upset and intimidate their readership.

An example of this can be found in "A Town of Memories", published in 1919 in Grand Magazine, in which he uses his well rehearsed romantic story with a slight shift of emphasis to explore his own return from the war and the general reception which soldiers received on their return. Following a young officer as he returns to the town in which he grew up, Burrage portrays an almost hostile environment into which he returns; he is unrecognised, and nobody pays any interest, respect or attention to him or his stories of the war, nor even to his reception of the Distinguished Service Order. Instead, the people of the town have their own interests and priorities with which to concern themselves. Though this contentious portrayal of post-war society certainly marks a slight shift in Burrage's writing, he returns to the romantic convention expected of him by reuniting the officer with a beautiful girl who had admired him throughout school. It would be harsh to not accept that market conditions expected one thing and to ignore them would mean turning his back on publications who still clamoured for his penmanship.

Another of Burrage's alternative directions is to be found in "The Recurring Tragedy", in which a General whose war tactics of attrition had been to the slaughtered cost of his soldiers, and he comes to re-imagine his own past as a Judas figure in a terrible vision. The Strange Career of Captain Dorry became a series for Lloyd's Magazine in 1920 about a gentleman crook and an ex-officer with a Military Cross who, idle in peacetime, meets a mysterious man called Fewgin whose business is in stolen goods and mind reading. Fewgin realises Dorry is a suitable candidate for recruitment into his gang of like-minded ex-military thieves, stealing only from "certain vampires who made money out of the war, and, by keeping up prices, are continuing to make money out of the peace". Again, in this motive, we see a glimpse of Burrage's own feelings on the war, as there is undoubtedly a bitterness towards those profiting from the suffering of others in such a manner. Fewgin justifies himself, saying:

"I help brave men who cannot help themselves. I give them a chance to get back a little of their own from the men who battened and fattened on them, who helped to starve their dependents while they were fighting, who smoked fat cigars in the haunts of their betters, and hoped the war might never end."

Burrage began to see slightly more success in the 1920s, achieving a couple of hard back publications entitled Some Ghost Stories and Poor Dear Esme. The latter, a comedy, concerns a boy who, for various reasons, is forced to disguise himself as a girl. Though these hard cover publications were a notable achievement, and one of which he was proud, the fact was that there was less money in it than in the magazines. In his history of the Strand Magazine, Reginald Pound portrays Burrage around this time, likening him to his equally prolific contemporary Herbert Shaw, considering them "two Bohemian temperaments that suffused and at times confused gifts from which more was expected than come forth. They had a precise knowledge of the popular short story as the product of calculated design. Both privately despised it, though it was their living."

The early 1920s, and with them a boom in prosperity, hope and happiness, now brought with them an increase in demand for war stories. Rather than preferring to ignore the atrocities of the war, which had seemed the general attitude in the immediate post-war years, society became more interested and concerned with the manner in which the war was fought, and the greed and political battles which had necessitated such bloodshed. Burrage answered this demand in 1930 with his own epochal piece, War Is War. He published under the pseudonym 'Ex-Private X', saying "were it otherwise I could not tell the truth about myself", though its publisher, Victor Gollancz, "who published the book and greatly admired it, had to point out that the critics would hardly take the book seriously if it became known that the author earned his living producing two or three slushy love stories a week".

In one of a series of letters he wrote to his contemporary and fellow writer Dorothy Sayers, Burrage bemoans how War is War "promised to be a great success, but was only a moderate one". The book itself was received with reviews on both sides of the spectrum. Cyril Fall's War Books, a survey of post-war writing published in 1930, gives a clear indication as to why the critics were so mixed in reception of the book. He writes:

This book is extremely uneven in quality. The account of the attack at Paschendaele and of conditions at Cambrai after the great German counter-attack are very good indeed; in fact among the best of their kind. But the rest is disfigured by an unreasoned and unpleasant attack on superiors and all troops other than those of the front line, which is all the more astonishing because the author is inclined to harp upon his social position as compared with that of many of the officers with whom he came in contact. He does not use as much bad language as many writers on the War, but his methods of abuse will leave on some of his readers at least a worse impression than the most highly-spiced language.

Dorothy Sayers was the editor at Victor Gollanz for anthologies of ghost and horror stories which included stories by Burrage. She says, in one of her letters of Burrage's story The Waxwork, a piece beyond the nerves of the editors, "what you say about "The Waxwork" sounds very exciting, just the sort of thing I want. Our nerves are stronger than those of the editors of periodicals, and we will publish anything, so long as it does not bring us into conflict with the Home Secretary". Though their correspondence began as strictly business, Burrage's acquaintance with Atherton Fleming, Sayers's husband, allowed their interactions to become less formal and friendlier. Burrage wrote of Fleming "I hope to encounter him soon in one of the Fleet Street tea-shops". 'Tea-shop' being a popular euphemism for the pub, where both Burrage and Fleming could frequently be found, though their alcohol consumption came to damage both their health and their professions, with Burrage coming off the worse.

Happily for Burrage, as a result of being featured in one of Sayers's anthologies, The Waxwork became one of his best-known stories and it would grab the attention of the film companies several times down the years even becoming an episode in the TV series 'Alfred Hitchcock Presents'.

The developing friendship between Burrage and Sayers enabled him to reveal more details of his personal life, admitting to her his "neuritis at both ends (legs and eyes)", and hinting at his troubles with alcohol: "Fleet Street is not a good place for a man who delights in succumbing to temptation, and whose doctor says that even small doses of alcohol are poison to him". Sayers sympathises, replying that Fleming "agrees with you entirely about the temptations of Fleet Street; he has, however, succeeded, through sheer strength of character, in being able to drink soda-water in the face of all his fellow journalists".

In another of Burrage's letters, he apologises for a delay in sending proofs of a story, with the words:

I have had a pretty thin time lately through illness and anxiety. And for days on end haven't had the energy in me to write a letter, and when I had the energy to send a complete set of proofs to you I found I hadn't the postage money (This is when you take out your handkerchief and start sobbing). I owed my late agent over £1000, so I got practically nothing out of War is War. He stuck to it. Well, he is paid off now, and so are my arrears of income tax. All this took a toll of my very small earning capacity, and I have been sold up. This on top of something which promised to be a great success and was only a moderate one, was a bit too much for me. Still, in spite of sickness I am resilient and shall float again. "You can't keep a good man down," as the whale said about Jonah.

For a man who had so many stories in so many magazines, and was gaining pace in Sayers's anthologies as a talented writer of horror stories, his income will have been far higher than the then average wage, and yet as he says, he finds himself short of money.

Several questions are left unanswered about his personal life. It is unclear whether he was still supporting family, or whether he spent the majority of his money on alcohol, or whether he chose to conceal his true fortunes from those around him. Perhaps most incongruous is the apparent absence of a wife; though his death certificate indicates that he had one, listed as H.A. Burrage, he seems never to mention her to Sayers.

He was around forty-two when he wrote that apology letter to Sayers, though in tone and circumstance it seems to be from a man in a far later stage of his life.

Burrage continued writing until his death in 1956, and continued to be prolifically published. Indeed, the Evening News alone published some forty of his stories between 1950-56. His death is recorded at Edgware General Hospital on 18th December, and the causes of his death are recorded as congestive cardiac failure, arteriosclerosis and chronic bronchitis. He was sixty-seven years old, and his last address is listed as 105 Vaughan Road, Harrow.

Though his name is not often remembered in lists of prominent writers of his time, or even it's genres, his ghost stories are highly regarded by critics and fans alike, while his life story tells us much about the trials and stresses placed on authors during and after the war, and on soldiers returning from that war. His reluctant acceptance that the money was in the magazines while the esteem was in the poorly-paying hard covers, and his persistence as a writer, speak of a determined man, doomed to circumstance yet living as best he could.

In ending A.M Burrage wrote a few sentences which best sum up two things. Firstly his love for his son Simon (who sadly passed away in October 2013 and was a great and passionate advocate for his Father's works.) and secondly his succinct reasons for writing.

TO JULIAN SIMON FIELD BURRAGE
who at the moment of writing will
soon achieve the great age of four.
From somebody who loves him.

In War is War I admitted being a professional writer, or in other words one who depends for his bread and cheese and beer on writing, typing or dictating strings of sentences which his masters, the Public, are kind enough to buy and presumably to read.

The book brought me letters from a few old friends and a great many new ones. A large percentage of the new friends, who missed having seen that my identity was rather unkindly betrayed by the Press, wrote and asked (a) who I was and (b) what sort of stories did I write?

The answer to the second question will be found in the following pages. The answer to the first question is 'Nobody Much', worse luck.

Most of these stories were written with the intention of giving the reader a pleasant shudder, in the hope that he will take a lighted candle to bed with him—for candle-makers must be considered in these hard times. Some have already made their bow from the pages of the monthly magazines. The best have, quite naturally, been rejected.